Little Birds

WORKS BY ANAÏS NIN

PUBLISHED BY THE SWALLOW PRESS

D. H. Lawrence: An Unprofessional Study
House of Incest (a prose poem)
Winter of Artifice
Under a Glass Bell (stories)
Ladders to Fire
Children of the Albatross
The Four-Chambered Heart
A Spy in the House of Love
Solar Barque
Seduction of the Minotaur
Collages
Cities of the Interior
A Woman Speaks

PUBLISHED BY HARCOURT BRACE JOVANOVICH

The Diary of Anaïs Nin, 1931–1934
The Diary of Anaïs Nin, 1934–1939
The Diary of Anaïs Nin, 1939–1944
The Diary of Anaïs Nin, 1944–1947
The Diary of Anaïs Nin, 1947–1955
The Diary of Anaïs Nin, 1955–1966
A Photographic Supplement to the Diary of Anaïs Nin
In Favor of the Sensitive Man and Other Essays
Delta of Venus: Erotica by Anaïs Nin
Linotte: The Early Diary of Anaïs Nin, 1914–1920
Little Birds: Erotica by Anaïs Nin

PUBLISHED BY MACMILLAN

The Novel of the Future

Little Birds

Erotica by Anaïs Nin

Harcourt Brace Jovanovich

New York and London

Contents

Preface
ix

Little Birds
1

The Woman on the Dunes
9

CONTENTS *viii*

Lina
21

Two Sisters
29

Sirocco
45

The Maja
53

A Model
61

The Queen
91

Hilda and Rango
99

The Chanchiquito
109

Saffron
117

Mandra
125

Runaway
135

Preface*

It is an interesting fact that very few writers have of their own accord sat down to write erotic tales or confessions. Even in France, where it is believed that the erotic has such an important role in life, the writers who did so were driven by necessity—the need of money.

It is one thing to include eroticism in a novel or a story and quite another to focus one's whole attention on it. The first is like life itself. It is, I might say, natural, sincere, as in the sensual pages of Zola or of Lawrence. But focusing wholly on the sexual life is not natural. It becomes something like the life of the prostitute, an abnormal activity that ends by turning the prostitute away from the sexual. Writers perhaps know this. That is why they have written only one confession or a few stories, on the side, to satisfy their honesty about life, as Mark Twain did.

But what happens to a group of writers who need money so badly that they devote themselves entirely to the erotic? How does this affect their lives, their feelings towards the world, their writing? What effect has it on their sexual life?

Let me explain that I was the mother confessor for such a group. In New York everything becomes harder, more cruel. I had many people to take care of, many problems, and since I was in character very much like George Sand, who wrote all night to take care of her children, lovers, friends, I had to find work. I became what I shall call the Madame of an unusual house of literary prostitution. It was a very artistic *"maison,"* I must say, a one-room studio with skylights, which I painted to look like pagan cathedral windows.

Before I took up my new profession I was known as a poet, as a woman who was independent and wrote only for her own pleasure. Many young writers, poets, came to me. We often collaborated, discussed and shared the work in progress. Varied as they were in character, inclinations, habits and vices, all the writers had one trait in common; they were poor. Desperately poor. Very often my *"maison"* was turned into a cafeteria where they dropped in, hungry, saying nothing, and we ate Quaker Oats because that was the cheapest thing to make, and it was said to give strength.

Most of the erotica was written on empty stomachs. Now, hunger is very good for stimulating the imagination; it does not produce sexual power, and sexual power does not produce unusual adventures. The more hunger, the greater the desires, like those of men in prison, wild and haunting. So we had here a perfect world in which to grow the flower of eroticism.

Of course, if you get too hungry, too continuously, you become a bum, a tramp. Those men who sleep along the East River, in doorways, on the Bowery, they have no sexual life at all, it is said. My writers—some of them lived in the Bowery—had not reached that stage yet.

As for me, my real writing was put aside when I set out in search of the erotic. These are my adventures in that world of prostitution. To bring them into the light was at first difficult. The sexual life is usually enveloped in many layers, for all of us—poets, writers, artists. It is a veiled woman, half-dreamed.

Little Birds

Manuel and his wife were poor, and when they first looked for an apartment in Paris, they found only two dark rooms below the street level, giving on to a small stifling courtyard. Manuel was sad. He was an artist, and there was no light in which he could work. His wife did not care. She would go off each day to do her trapeze act for the circus.

In that dark under-the-earth place, his whole life assumed the character of an imprisonment. The concierges were extremely old, and the tenants who lived in the house seemed to have agreed to make it an old people's home.

So Manuel wandered through the streets until he came to a sign: FOR RENT. He was led to two attic rooms that looked like a hovel, but one of the rooms led to a terrace, and as Manuel stepped out onto this terrace he was greeted with the shouts of schoolgirls on recess. There was a school across the way, and the girls were playing in the yard under the terrace.

Manuel watched them for a few moments, his face glowing and expanding in a smile. He was taken with a slight trembling, like that of a man anticipating great pleasures. He wanted to move into the apartment immediately, but when evening came and he persuaded Thérèse to come and inspect it, she saw nothing but two uninhabitable rooms, dirty and neglected. Manuel repeated, "But there is light, there is light for painting, and there is a terrace." Thérèse shrugged her shoulders and said, "I wouldn't live here."

Then Manuel became crafty. He bought paint, cement and wood. He rented the two rooms and devoted himself to fixing them. He had never liked work, yet this time he set about doing the most meticulous carpentry and paint job ever seen, to make the place beautiful for Thérèse. As he painted, patched, cemented and hammered, he could hear the laughter of the little girls playing in the yard. But he contained himself, waiting for the right moment. He spun fantasies of what his life would be in this apartment across from a girls' school.

In two weeks the place was transformed. The walls were white, the doors closed properly, the closets could be used, the floors no longer had holes in them. Then he brought Thérèse to see it. She was quite overwhelmed and immediately agreed to move. In one day their belongings were brought on a cart. In this new place, Manuel said, he could paint because of the light. He was dancing about, gay and changed.

Thérèse was happy to see him in such a mood. The next morning, when things were but half-unpacked and they had slept on beds without sheets, Thérèse went to her trapeze work and Manuel was left alone to arrange things. But instead of unpacking he went downstairs and walked to the bird market. There he spent the grocery money that Thérèse had given him to buy a cage and two tropical birds. He went home and hung the cage outside on the terrace. He looked down for a moment at the little girls playing, watching their legs under the fluttering skirts. How they fell upon each other in games, how their hair flew behind as they ran! Their tiny new breasts were already beginning to show in their very plumpness. His face was flushed, but he did not linger. He had a plan, and it was too perfect to surrender now. For three days he spent the food money on birds of every kind. The terrace was now alive with birds.

Each morning at ten o'clock Thérèse was off to work, and the apartment was filled with sunlight and the laughter and cries of little girls.

The fourth day Manuel stepped out on the terrace. Ten o'clock was the recreation hour. The schoolyard was animated. To Manuel it was an orgy of legs and very short skirts, which revealed white panties during the games. He was growing feverish, standing there among his birds, but finally the plan succeeded; the girls looked up.

Manuel called, "Why don't you come and see? There are birds from all over the world. There is even a bird from Brazil with the head of a monkey."

The girls laughed, but after school, impelled by curiosity, several of them ran up to his apartment. Manuel was afraid that Thérèse would come in. So he just let them watch the birds and be amused by their colored beaks and antics and odd cries. He let them chatter and look, familiarize themselves with the place.

By the time Thérèse came at one-thirty, he had won from the girls the promise that they would come and see him the next day at noon as soon as school was over.

At the appointed hour they arrived to watch the birds, four little girls of all sizes—one with long blond hair, another with curls, the third plump and languid and the fourth slender and shy, with big eyes.

As they stood there watching the birds, Manuel became more and more nervous and excited. He said, "Excuse me, I have to go and pee."

He left the door of the toilet open so that they could see him. Only one of them, the shy one, turned her face and fixed her eyes on him. Manuel had his back to the girls but looked over his shoulder to see if they were watching him. When he noticed the shy girl, with her enormous eyes, she glanced away. Manuel was obliged to button himself up. He wanted to have his pleasure cautiously. That was enough for today.

Having seen the big eyes upon him set him dreaming for the rest of the day, offering his restless penis to the mirror, shaking it like a candy or a fruit or a gift.

Manuel was well aware that he was highly endowed by nature in the matter of size. If it was true that his penis wilted as soon as he came too close to a woman, as soon as he lay at a woman's side; if it was true that it failed him whenever he wanted to give Thérèse what she wanted, it was equally true that if a woman looked at him, it would grow to enormous proportion and behave in the most vivacious way. It was then that he was at his best.

During the hours when the girls were shut in their classrooms he would frequent the *pissoirs* of Paris, of which there were so many—the little round kiosks, the labyrinths without doors, out of which would always come men boldly buttoning themselves while staring straight into the face of a very elegant woman, a perfumed and chic woman, who would not be immediately aware that the man was coming out of a *pissoir* and who would then drop her eyes. This was one of Manuel's greatest delights.

He would also stand there against the urinal and look up at the houses above his head, where often there would be a woman leaning out of a window or standing on a balcony, and from up there they would see him holding his penis. He derived no pleasure from being stared at by men or else this would have been a paradise for him, for all men knew the trick of pissing away quietly while looking at his neighbor performing the same operation. And young boys would come in for no other reason but to see and perhaps help each other along in the act.

The day when the shy girl had looked at Manuel he was very happy. He thought that now it would be easier to satisfy himself fully if only he could control himself. What he feared was the impetuous desire that took hold of him to show himself no matter what the cost, and then all would be spoiled.

This was the moment for another visit, and the little girls were coming up the stairs. Manuel had donned a kimono, one that could easily slip open, by accident.

The birds were performing quite beautifully, bickering and kissing and quarreling. Manuel stood behind the girls. Suddenly his kimono opened, and when he found himself touching long blond hair, he lost his head. Instead of wrapping his kimono, he opened it wider, and as the girls turned they all saw him standing there in a trance, his big penis erect, pointing at them. They all took fright, like little birds, and ran away.

The Woman on the Dunes

Louis could not sleep. He turned over in his bed to lie on his stomach and, burying his face in the pillow, moved against the hot sheets as if he were lying over the woman. But when the friction increased the fever in his body, he stopped himself.

He got out of bed and looked at his watch. It was two

o'clock. What could he do to appease his fever? He left his studio. The moon was shining and he could see the roads clearly. The place, a beach town in Normandy, was full of little cottages, which people could rent for a night or a week. Louis wandered aimlessly.

Then he saw that one of the cottages was lighted. It was set into the woods, isolated. It intrigued him that anyone should be up so late. He approached it soundlessly, his footsteps lost in the sand. The Venetian blinds were down but not tightly closed, so he could see right into the room. And his eyes met with the most amazing sight: a very wide bed, profusely covered with pillows and rumpled blankets, as if it already had been the scene of a great battle; a man, seemingly cornered in a pile of pillows, as if pushed there after a series of attacks, reclining like a pasha in a harem, very calm and contented, naked, his legs folded out; and a woman, also naked, whom Louis could see only from the back, contorting herself before this pasha, undulating and deriving such pleasure from whatever she was doing with her head between his legs that her ass would shake tremulously, her legs tighten as if she were about to leap.

Now and then the man placed his hand over her head as if to restrain her frenzy. He tried to move away. Then she leaped with great agility and placed herself over him, kneeling over his face. He no longer moved. His face was directly under her sex, which, her stomach curved outwards, she held before him.

As he was pinned under her, she was the one to move within reach of his mouth, which had not touched her yet. Louis saw the man's sex rise and lengthen, and he tried with an embrace to bring her down upon him. But she remained at a short distance, looking, enjoying the spectacle of her own beautiful stomach and hair and sex so near to his mouth.

Then slowly, slowly she moved towards him and, with her

head bowed, watched the melting of his mouth between her legs.

For a long while they maintained this position. Louis was in such a turmoil that he left the window. Had he remained longer he would have had to throw himself on the ground and somehow satisfy his burning desire, and this he did not want to do.

He began to feel that in every cottage something was taking place that he would like to be sharing. He walked faster, haunted by the image of the man and woman, the round firm belly of the woman as she arched herself over the man . . .

Then he reached the sand dunes and complete solitude. The dunes shone like snowy hills in the clear night. Behind them lay the ocean, whose rhythmic movements he could hear. He walked in the white moonlight. And then he caught sight of a figure walking before him, walking fast and lightly. It was a woman. She wore some kind of cape, which the wind billowed like a sail, and seemed propelled by it. He would never catch up with her.

She was walking towards the ocean. He followed her. They walked in the snowlike dunes for a long while. At the ocean's edge, she flung off her clothes and stood naked in the summer night. She ran into the surf. And Louis, in imitation, discarded his clothes and ran into the water also. Only then did she see him. At first she was still. But when she saw his young body clearly in the moonlight, his fine head, his smile, she was not frightened. He swam towards her. They smiled at each other. His smile, even at night, was dazzling; hers, too. They could scarcely distinguish anything but the brilliant smiles and the outlines of their perfect bodies.

He came closer to her. She let him. Suddenly he swam deftly and gracefully over her body, touching it, and passing on.

She continued to swim, and he repeated his passage over

her. Then she stood up, and he dove down and passed between her legs. They laughed. They both moved with ease in the water.

He was deeply excited. He swam with his sex hard. Then they approached each other with a crouching motion, as if for a battle. He brought her body against his, and she felt the tautness of his penis.

He placed it between her legs. She touched it. His hands searched her, caressed her everywhere. Then again she moved away, and he had to swim to catch her. Again his penis lay lightly between her legs, then he pressed her more firmly against him and sought to penetrate her. She broke loose and ran out of the water, into the sand dunes. Dripping, shining, laughing, he ran after her. The warmth of the running set him on fire again. She fell on the sand, and he over her.

Then at the moment when he most desired her, his power suddenly failed him. She lay waiting for him, smiling and moist, and his desire wilted. Louis was baffled. He had been in a state of desire for days. He wanted to take this woman and he couldn't. He was deeply humiliated.

Strangely enough, her voice grew tender. "There is plenty of time," she said. "Don't move away. It's lovely."

Her warmth passed into him. His desire did not return, but it was sweet to feel her. Their bodies lay together, his belly against hers, his sexual hair brushing against hers, her breasts pointed against his chest, her mouth glued to his.

Then slowly he slipped off to look at her—her long, slender, polished legs, her rich pubic hair, her lovely pale glowing skin, her full breasts very high, her long hair, her wide smiling mouth.

He was sitting like a Buddha. She leaned over and took his small wilted penis in her mouth. She licked it softly, tenderly, lingering over the tip of it. It stirred.

He looked down at the sight of her wide red mouth so

beautifully curved around his penis. With one hand she touched his balls, with the other she moved the head of the penis, enclosing it and pulling it gently.

Then, sitting against him, she took it and directed it between her legs. She rubbed the penis gently against her clitoris, over and over again. Louis watched the hand, thinking how beautiful it looked, holding the penis as if it were a flower. It stirred but did not harden sufficiently to enter her.

He could see at the opening of her sex the moisture of her desire appearing, glistening in the moonlight. She continued to rub. The two bodies, equally beautiful, were bent over this rubbing motion, the small penis feeling the touch of her skin, her warm flesh, enjoying the friction.

She said, "Give me your tongue," and leaned over. Without interrupting the rubbing of his penis, she took his tongue into her mouth and touched the tip of it with her own tongue. Each time the penis touched her clitoris, her tongue touched the tip of his tongue. And Louis felt the warmth running between his tongue and his penis, running back and forth.

In a husky voice she said, "Stick your tongue out, out."

He obeyed her. She again cried, "Out, out, out, out . . ." obsessively, and when he did so he felt such a stirring through his body, as if it were his penis extending towards her, to reach into her.

She kept her mouth open, two slender fingers around his penis, her legs parted, expectantly.

Louis felt a turmoil, the blood running through his body and down to his penis. It hardened.

The woman waited. She did not take in his penis at once. She let him, now and then, touch his tongue against her. She let him pant like a dog in heat, open his being, stretch towards her. He looked at the red mouth of her sex, open and waiting, and suddenly the violence of his desire shook him, completed the hardening of his penis. He threw himself over her, his tongue inside of her mouth, and his penis pressing inside of her.

But again he could not come. They rolled together for a long while. Finally they got up and walked, carrying their clothes. Louis' sex was stretched and taut, and she delighted in the sight. Now and then they fell on the sand, and he took her, and churned her, and left her, moist and hot. And as they again walked, she in front of him, he encircled her in his arms, and threw her on the ground so that they were like dogs coupling, on their hands and knees. He shook inside of her, pushed and vibrated, and kissed her, and held her breasts in his hands.

"Do you want it? Do you want it?" he asked.

"Yes, give it to me, but make it last, do not come; I like it like this, over and over and over again."

She was so moist and feverish. She would walk, waiting for the moment he would thrust her into the sand and take her again, stirring her and then leaving her before she had come. Each time, she felt anew his hands over her body, the warm sand against her skin, his caressing mouth, the caressing wind.

As they walked, she took his erect penis into her hand. Once she stopped him, knelt before him and held it in her mouth. He stood towering over her, with his belly moving slightly forwards. Another time she pressed his penis between her breasts, making a cushion for it, holding it and letting it glide between this soft embrace. Dizzy, palpitating, vibrating from these caresses, they walked drunkenly.

Then they saw a house and stopped. He begged her to conceal herself among the bushes. He wanted to come; he would not leave her until then. She was so aroused and yet she wanted to hold back and wait for him.

This time when he was inside of her he began shaking,

and finally he came, with a violence. She half climbed over his body to reach her own fulfillment. They cried together.

Lying back, resting, smoking, with the dawn coming upon them, lighting their faces, they now felt too cool and covered their bodies with their clothes. The woman, looking away from Louis, told him a story.

She had been in Paris when they had hanged a Russian radical who had killed a diplomat. She was then living in Montparnasse, frequenting the cafés, and she had followed the trial with a passion, as all her friends had done, because the man was a fanatic, had given Dostoevskian answers to the questions put to him, faced the trial with great religious courage.

At that time they still executed people for grave offenses. It usually took place at dawn, when no one was about, in a little square near the prison of the Santé, where the guillotine had stood at the time of the Revolution. And one could not get very near, because of the police guard. Few people attended these hangings. But in the case of the Russian, because emotions had been so much aroused, all the students and artists of Montparnasse, the young agitators and revolutionaries had decided to attend. They waited up all night, getting drunk.

She had waited with them, had drunk with them, and was in a great state of excitement and fear. It was the first time she was to see someone die. It was the first time she was to see someone hanged. It was the first time she was to witness a scene that had been repeated many, many times during the Revolution.

Towards dawn, the crowd moved to the square, as near as the rope, stretched by the policemen, would allow and gathered in a circle. She was carried by the waves of crowding and pushing people to a spot about ten meters away from the scaffold.

There she stood, pressed against the rope, watching with fascination and terror. Then a stirring in the crowd pushed her away from her position. Still, she could see by standing on her toes. People were crushing her from all sides. The prisoner was brought in with his eyes blindfolded. The hangman stood by, waiting. Two policemen held the man and slowly led him up the stairs of the scaffold.

At this moment she became aware of someone pressing against her far more eagerly than necessary. In the trembling, excited condition she was in, the pressure was not disagreeable. Her body was in a fever. Anyway, she could scarcely move, so pinned was she to the spot by the curious crowd.

She wore a white blouse and a skirt that buttoned all the way down the side as was the fashion then—a short skirt and a blouse through which one could see her rosy underwear and guess at the shape of her breasts.

Two hands encircled her waist, and she distinctly felt a man's body, his desire hard against her ass. She held her breath. Her eyes were fixed on the man who was about to be hanged, which made her body painfully nervous, and at the same time the hands reached for her breasts and pressed upon them.

She felt dizzy with conflicting sensations. She did not move or turn her head. A hand now sought an opening in the skirt and discovered the buttons. Each button undone by the hand made her gasp with both fear and relief. The hand waited to see if she protested before proceeding to another button. She did not move.

Then with a dexterity and swiftness she had not expected, the two hands twisted her skirt round so that the opening was at the back. In the heaving crowd, now all she could feel was a penis slowly being slipped into the opening of her skirt.

Her eyes remained fixed on the man who was mounting the scaffold, and with each beat of her heart the penis gained headway. It had traversed the skirt and parted the slit in her panties. How warm and firm and hard it was against her flesh. The condemned man stood on the scaffold now and the noose was put around his neck. The pain of watching him was so great that it made this touch of flesh a relief, a human, warm, consoling thing. It seemed to her then that this penis quivering between her buttocks was something wonderful to hold on to, life, life to hold while death was passing . . .

Without saying a word, the Russian bowed his head in the noose. Her body trembled. The penis advanced between the soft folds of her buttocks, pushed its way inexorably into her flesh.

She was palpitating with fear, and it was like the palpitation of desire. As the condemned man was flung into space and death, the penis gave a great leap inside of her, gushing out its warm life.

The crowd crushed the man against her. She almost ceased breathing, and as her fear became pleasure, wild pleasure at feeling life while a man was dying, she fainted.

After this story Louis dozed off to sleep. When he awakened, saturated with sensual dreams, vibrating from some imaginary embrace, he saw that the woman had gone. He could follow her footprints along the sand for quite a distance, but they disappeared in the wooded section that led to the cottages, and so he lost her.

Lina

Lina is a liar who cannot bear her real face in the mirror. She has a face that proclaims her sensuality, lightning in her eyes, an avid mouth, a provocative glance. But instead of yielding to her eroticism, she is ashamed of it. She throttles it. And all this desire, lust, gets twisted inside of her and churns a poison of envy and jealousy. Whenever sensuality shows its blossom, Lina hates it. She is jealous of everything, of everybody else's loves. She is jealous when she sees couples kissing in the streets of Paris, in the cafés, in the park. She looks at them with a strange look of anger. She wishes nobody would make love because she can't do it.

She bought herself a black lace nightgown like mine. She came to my apartment to spend a few nights with me. She said she had bought the nightgown for a lover, but I saw the price tag still fastened on it. She was ravishing to look at because she was plump and her breasts showed where her white blouse opened. I saw her wild mouth parted, her curly hair in a wild aureole around her head. Every gesture was one of disorder and violence, as if a lioness had come into the room.

She began by asserting that she hated my lovers, Hans and Michel. "Why?" I said. "Why?" Her reasons were confused, inadequate. I was sad. That meant secret meetings with them. How could I amuse Lina while she stayed in Paris? What did she want?

"Just to be with you."

So we were reduced to each other's company. We sat at cafés, we shopped, we strolled.

I liked to see her dress up for the evening in barbaric jewelry, her face so vivid. She was not for gentle Paris, for the cafés. She was meant for the African jungle, orgies, dances. But she was not a free being, rippling in natural undulations of pleasure and desire. If her mouth, body, voice, were made for sensuality, its true flow was paralyzed in her. Between her legs she was impaled on a rigid pole of puritanism. All the rest of her body was loose, provocative. She always looked as if she had just come from lying in bed with a lover, or as if she were just about to lie down with one. She had circles under her eyes and such a great restlessness, an energy smoking from her whole body, impatience, avidity.

She did everything to seduce me. She liked our kissing on

the mouth. She held my mouth, and excited herself, and then drew away. We had breakfast together. She lay in bed and raised her leg so that from where I was sitting at the foot of the bed I could see her sex. While she dressed she dropped her chemise, pretending that she had not heard me come in, and stood naked for a moment, then covered herself.

The nights when Hans came to see me there was always a scene. She had to sleep then in the room above mine. The next morning she would awaken sick with jealousy. She made me kiss her on the mouth again and again until we got excited, and then she stopped. She liked those kisses without climax.

We went out together and I admired the woman who was singing in the little café. Lina got drunk and was furious with me. She said, "If I were a man, I would murder you."

I became angry. Then she wept and said, "Don't abandon me. If you abandon me I am lost."

At the same time she raved against Lesbianism, saying it was revolting, and would not permit anything but the kissing. Her scenes were wearing me out.

When Hans saw her he said, "The trouble with Lina is that she is a man."

I told myself that I would try and find out, break her resistance in some way or another. I was never very good at wooing people who resisted. I wanted them to want it, to be yielding.

When Hans and I were in my bedroom at night, we were afraid to make a noise that she might hear. I did not want to hurt her, but I hated her scenes of frustration and her negative jealousy.

"What do you want, Lina, what do you want?"

"I want you not to have lovers. I hate it when I see you with men."

"Why do you hate men so?"

"They have something I don't have. I want to have a penis so that I can make love to you."

"There are other ways of making love between women."

"But I won't have it, I won't have it."

Then one day I said, "Why don't you come with me and visit Michel? I want you to see his explorer's den."

Michel had said to me, "Bring her, I will hypnotize her. You will see."

She consented. We went up to his apartment. He had been burning incense, but an incense I did not know.

Lina was quite nervous when she saw his place. The erotic atmosphere disturbed her. She sat down on the fur-covered couch. She looked like a beautiful animal, one well worth capturing. I could see that Michel wanted to dominate her. The incense was making us slightly drowsy. Lina wanted to open the window. But Michel came over and sat between us and began talking to her.

His voice was gentle and enveloping. He was telling stories of his voyages. I saw that Lina was listening, that she had ceased twitching and smoking feverishly, that she was lying back and dreaming over his endless stories. Her eyes were half-closed. Then she fell asleep.

"What did you do, Michel?" I felt quite drowsy myself.

He smiled, "I burned a Japanese incense that makes one sleepy. It's an aphrodisiac. It is not harmful." He was smiling mischievously. I laughed.

Lina was not altogether asleep. She had crossed her knees. Michel climbed over her and tried to open them gently with his hands, but they remained tightly closed. Then he inserted his own knee between her thighs and parted them. I was roused by the sight of Lina so yielding and open now. I began caressing her, undressing her. She knew what I was doing but she was enjoying it. She kept her mouth on mine and her eyes closed and let Michel and me undress her completely.

Her rich breasts covered Michel's face. He bit the nipples. She let Michel kiss her between the legs and insert his penis, and she let me kiss her breasts and caress them. She had wonderful firm round buttocks. Michel kept pushing her legs apart and biting into her soft flesh until she began to moan. She would have nothing but the penis. So Michel took her and when she had enjoyed him he wanted to take me. She sat up, opened her eyes and watched us wonderingly for a moment, then took Michel's penis out of me and would not let him insert it again. She threw herself on me with a sexual fury, caressing me with her mouth and her hands. Michel took her again from behind.

When we came out on the street, Lina and I, holding each other by the waist, she pretended not to remember anything that had happened. I let her. The next day she left Paris.

Two Sisters

There were two young sisters. One was stocky, dark-haired, vivid. The other was graceful, delicate. Dorothy had strength. Edna had a beautiful voice that haunted people, and she wanted to be an actress. They came from a well-to-do family who lived in Maryland. In the cellar of their house their father made a ceremony of burning D. H. Lawrence's books, which betrays how far behind this family was in the development of the sensual life. In spite of this, their father, with his eyes wet and brilliant, liked to take the girls on his knees, slip his hand under their little dresses and caress them.

They had two brothers, Jake and David. Before the boys could get an erection they played at making love with their sisters. David and Dorothy were always paired off together, as were Edna and Jake. The delicate David liked his husky sister, and the rather virile Jake liked the plantlike fragility of Edna. The brothers laid their soft young penises between their sisters' legs, but that was all. This was done in great secrecy, lying on the rug of the dining room and accompanied by a feeling that they were committing the greatest of sexual crimes.

Then suddenly these games stopped. The boys had discovered the world of sex through another boy. The sisters became self-conscious and were growing up. Puritanism was asserting itself in the family. Their father thundered and fought each intrusion from the outside world. He growled at the young men who came to call. He growled at dances, at parties of all kinds. With the fanaticism of an inquisitor, he burned the books he found his children reading. He gave up caressing his daughters. He did not know that they had made slits in their panties so when they dated they could be kissed between the legs, that they sat in cars with boys, sucking their penises, that the seat of the family car was stained with sperm. Even so, he fought off the young men who called too often. He did everything to prevent his daughters from marrying.

Dorothy was studying sculpture. Edna still wanted to go on the stage. But then she fell in love with a man older than herself, the first man she had really known. The others were boys to her; they aroused a sort of maternal craving in her, a desire to protect. But Harry was forty, and he worked for a

company that took rich people on cruises. As social captain of
the cruise, it was his job to see that the guests were enter-
tained, that they met one another, that their comforts were
complete—and their intrigues, too. He helped the husbands to
escape the vigilance of the wives, and the wives to escape
their husbands. His stories of trips with these pampered rich
stirred Edna.

They got married. They took a trip around the world together. What Edna discovered in their travels was that the social captain supplied a great deal of the sexual intrigue in
person.

Edna returned from the trip estranged from her husband.
Sexually he had not awakened her. She did not know why.
Sometimes she thought it was because of her discovery of his
having belonged to so many women. From the first night, it
seemed that his possession was not of her, but of a woman
like a hundred others. He had shown no emotion. When he
undressed her he had said, "Oh, you have such thick hips.
You seemed so slender, I never imagined you could have such
thick hips."

She felt humiliated, she felt that she was not desirable.
This paralyzed her own confidence, her own outflow of love
and desire for him. Partly in a mood of revenge, she began to
look at him just as coldly as he had looked at her, and what
she saw was a man of forty whose hair was growing thin, who
was soon going to be very fat and looked ready to retire into a
familiar and stolid life. He was no longer the man who had
seen all the world.

Then came Robert, thirty years old, dark-haired, with
burning brown eyes like some animal that looked at once hungry and tender. He was fascinated by Edna's voice, enchanted
by the softness of it. He was completely spellbound by her.

He had just won a scholarship with an acting company.
He and Edna shared a love of the stage. He renewed her faith

in herself, in her attractiveness. He was not even quite aware that it was love. He treated her somewhat like an older sister, until one day backstage, when everyone had gone home and Edna had been rehearsing him, listening to him, giving her impressions, they acted out a kiss that did not stop. He took her, on the sofa of the stage setting, awkwardly, hurriedly, but with such an intensity that she felt him as she had never felt her husband. His words of praise, worship, cries of wonder, incited her, and she bloomed in his hands. They fell on the floor. The dust got into their throats, but they were still kissing, caressing, and Robert had a second erection.

Edna and Robert were together all the time. Her alibi for Harry was that she was studying acting. It was a period of drunkenness, of blindness, of living only with the hands and mouth and body. Edna let Harry go off alone on his cruise. She was free now for six months. She and Robert lived together in New York, secretly. He had such magnetism in his hands that his touch, even his hand on her arm, sent warmth all through her. She lived open and sensitized to his presence. And his feeling about her voice was the same. He would telephone her at all hours to hear it. It was like a song luring him out of himself and out of his life. All other women were canceled by her voice.

He entered her love with a sense of absolute possession, security. To hide and sleep in her, take her, enjoy her, they were all the same. There were no tensions, no moments of ambivalence, hatred. The lovemaking never became wild and cruel, an animal bout in which one strives to rape the other, force one's way into the other and hurt with violence or desire. No, this was a melting together, a vanishing together into a soft, dark womb of warmth.

Harry returned. And at the same time Dorothy came back from the West, where she had been working, sculpturing. She was herself now like a piece of highly polished wood,

her features firm and chiseled, her voice earthy, her legs
sturdy, her very nature hard and strong, like the work she
did.

She saw what had happened to Edna but did not know
about her estrangement from Harry. She thought Robert had
caused it, and hated him. She assumed he was a lover of the
moment, just separating Harry and Edna for his own pleasure.
She did not believe it was love. She fought Robert. She was
cutting, biting. She herself was like an impregnable virgin,
though not puritanical or squeamish. She was open like a man,
used lusty words, told bawdy stories, laughed about sex. But
still she was impregnable to all.

She felt Robert's antagonism exultantly. She loved the fire
and angry demons in him, biting, snarling at her. What she
hated above all was that most men in her presence wilted,
grew small and feeble. Only the timid ones approached her,
as if to seek her strength. She wanted to shatter them, seeing
the way they crawled toward her treelike body. The idea of
letting them push their penis between her legs was like allow-
ing some insect to crawl over her. Whereas she gloried in the
struggle to push Robert out of Edna's life, to humiliate him,
demolish him. The three of them would sit together, Edna
hiding her feelings about Harry, Robert not offering to take
her away, not thinking, living only in the romantic present—
dreamer. Dorothy accused him of this. Edna defended him;
all the time she sat there thinking of the fiery way Robert took
her the first time, the narrow little couch on which they lay,
the dusty rug on which they rolled; thinking of his hands, the
way they penetrated her.

Edna said to her sister, "You cannot understand. You
have never been in love like this."

Then Dorothy was silenced.

The two sisters slept in adjoining rooms. There was a big

bathroom between the rooms. Harry had gone again for six months. Edna let Robert come to her room at night.

One morning looking out of the window, Dorothy saw Edna leave the house. She did not know that Robert was still in her room asleep. She went into the bathroom to take a bath. Edna had left her door open, and Dorothy, thinking herself alone, did not trouble to close it. On this door there was a mirror. Dorothy came into the bathroom and dropped her kimono. She pinned her hair up, she made up her face. Her body was magnificent. Every movement she made before the mirror brought out the provocative full, taut curves of her breasts and buttocks. Her hair was full of lights; she brushed it. Her breasts danced as she moved. She stood on her toes to make up her eyelashes.

And Robert, on awakening found himself looking at this spectacle from the bed, everything mirrored before him. Suddenly his whole body flushed with warmth. He threw off the covers. Dorothy was still visible in the mirror. She was leaning over to pick up her hairbrush. Robert could not bear any more. He went to the bathroom and stood there. Dorothy made no outcry. He was naked, his penis thrust out towards her, his brown eyes burning her.

As he made a step towards her, Dorothy was taken with a strange trembling. She felt herself craving to move towards him. They fell upon each other. He half dragged, half carried her to the bed. It was like the continuation of their struggle, for she fought him, but her every movement only made him increase the pressure of his knees, of his hands, of his mouth. Robert was wild with a desire to hurt, to bend her to his will, her resistance warming his muscles, his anger. As he took her, breaking through the virginity, he bit into her, adding pain. She was oblivious to it because of the effect of his body on hers. Wherever he touched her, she burned; after the initial pain it seemed as if her womb was inflamed too. When it was

over, she craved him again. It was she who took his penis between her hands and pushed it in again, and stronger than the
pain was the ecstasy of his moving inside of her.

Robert had discovered a stronger sensation, a stronger
flavor—the smell of Dorothy's hair, of her body, the strength
of her as she enclosed him. In one hour she had obliterated
his feelings for Edna.

Afterward, Dorothy was like one possessed as she remembered Robert lying over her body, moving up so that he could
rub his penis between her breasts, moving towards her mouth,
and she felt the dizziness one experiences before an abyss, a
sense of falling, of annihilation.

She did not know how to face Edna. She was torn with
jealousy. She was afraid Robert would try to keep them both.
But with Edna he only felt like becoming a child, lying at her
side, putting his head on her breast and confessing everything
to her, out of a need for a mother, not thinking at all of the
hurt it would cause her. But he realized he could not stay. He
invented a trip. He begged Dorothy to go with him. Dorothy
said that she would leave later. He went to London.

Edna followed him there. Dorothy went to Paris. She was
now trying to escape from Robert because of her love for
Edna. She began having an affair with a young American,
Donald, because he resembled Robert.

Robert wrote her that he could not make love to Edna
anymore, that he had to pretend all the time. He had found
out she was born the same day as his mother, and she was
becoming more and more identified with his mother, which
paralyzed him. He wouldn't tell her the truth.

Soon after, he went to Paris to meet Dorothy. She continued to see Donald, too. Then she and Robert went on a trip.
That week together, they thought they were going to go
crazy. Robert's caresses put Dorothy in such a state that she
begged "Take me!" He would pretend to refuse, just to see

her rolling in exquisite torture, on the verge of an orgasm and needing him only to touch her with the tip of his penis. Then she learned to tease him, too, to leave him when he was about to come. She would pretend to fall asleep. And he would lie there, tortured by the desire to be touched again, afraid to awaken her. He would edge close to her, place his penis against her ass, trying to move against it, to come just by touching her, but he couldn't, and then she would awaken and begin touching him and sucking him again. They did it so often that it became a torture. Her face was swollen from the kissing, and she had marks of his teeth on her body, and yet they could not touch each other in the street, even while walking, without jumping again with desire.

They decided to get married. Robert wrote to Edna.

On the day of the wedding, Edna came to Paris. Why? It was as if she wanted to see everything with her own eyes, to suffer the very last drop of bitterness. In a few days she had become an old woman. A month before she was glowing, enchanting, her voice like a song, like an aureole around her, her walk light, her smile inundating one. And now she wore a mask. Over this mask she had spread powder. There was no glow of life under it. Her hair was lifeless. The glaze in her eyes was like that of a dying person.

Dorothy was faint when she saw her. She cried out to her. Edna did not answer. She merely stared.

The wedding was ghostly. Donald burst in in the middle of it and behaved like a madman, threatening Dorothy for deceiving him, threatening to commit suicide. When it was over, Dorothy fainted. Edna stood there carrying flowers, a figure of death.

Robert and Dorothy left on a trip. They wanted to revisit the places they had traveled through a few weeks before, recapture the same pleasure. But when Robert tried to take Dorothy he found that she could not respond. Her body had undergone a change. The life had ebbed from it. He thought, It is the strain, the strain of having seen Edna, of the wedding, the scene made by Donald. So he was tender. He waited. Dorothy wept during the night. The next night it was the same. And the next. Robert tried caressing her, but her body did not vibrate under his fingers. Even her mouth did not answer his mouth. It was as though she had died. After a while she concealed it from him. She pretended to feel enjoyment. But when Robert was not looking at her, she looked exactly like Edna on the day of the wedding.

She kept her secret. Robert was deceived, until one day when they took a room in a rather cheap hotel, because the best ones were filled. The walls were thin, the doors did not close well. They got into bed. As soon as they put out the light they heard the springs of the bed in the next room squeaking rhythmically, two heavy bodies pounding into each other. Then the woman began to moan. Dorothy sat up in bed and sobbed for all that was lost.

Obscurely she felt what had happened to be a punishment. She knew it was related to her taking Robert from Edna. She thought she could recapture at least the physical response with other men, and perhaps free herself and return to Robert. When they went back to New York she sought adventures. In her head she was always hearing the moans and cries of the couple in the hotel room. She would not rest until she had felt this again. Edna could not cheat her of this, could not kill the life in her. It was too great a punishment for something that was not altogether her fault.

She tried to meet Donald again. But Donald had changed. He had hardened, crystallized. Once an emotional, impulsive young man, he had become completely objective, mature, searching for his pleasure.

"Of course," he said to Dorothy, "you know who is responsible for this. I would not have minded at all if you had discovered you didn't love me, left me, gone to Robert. I knew you were attracted to him, I didn't know how deeply. But I couldn't forgive your keeping us both at the same time, in Paris. I must have taken you often a few minutes after he had. You asked for violence. I didn't know you were asking me to surpass Robert, to try to efface him from your body. I thought you were merely in a frenzy of desire. So I responded. You know how I made love to you, I cracked your bones, I bent you, twisted you. Once I made you bleed. Then from me you would take a taxi and go to him. And you told me that after lovemaking you didn't wash because you liked the smell that went through your clothes, you liked the smells that followed you for a day after. I nearly went crazy when I discovered all this, I wanted to kill you."

"I have been sufficiently punished," said Dorothy violently.

Donald looked at her. "What do you mean?"

"Ever since I married Robert I have been frigid."

Donald's eyebrows lifted. Then his face set in an ironical expression. "And why do you tell me this? Do you expect me to make you bleed again? So that you can go back to your Robert all wet between the legs, and enjoy him at last? God knows I still love you. But my life is changed. I do not go in for love anymore."

"How do you live?"

"I have my little pleasures. I invite certain choice friends; I offer them drinks; they sit in my room—where you are sitting. Then I go into the kitchen to mix more drinks, and give them a little time alone. They already know my taste, my little predilections.

"When I come back . . . well, she may be sitting in your armchair with her skirt lifted, and he kneeling before her looking at her or kissing her, or he may be sitting in the chair and she . . .

"What I like is the surprise, and seeing them. They do not notice me. In a way, that is how it would have been with you and Robert if I could have witnessed your little scenes. Possibly a remembrance of some kind. Now if you like, you can wait for a few minutes. There is a friend coming. He is exceptionally attractive."

Dorothy wanted to leave. Then she observed something that made her stop. The door of Donald's bathroom was open. It was covered with a mirror. She turned to Donald and said: "Listen, I'll stay, but can I express a whim, too? One that will not in the least alter the satisfaction of yours."

"What is it?"

"Instead of going into the kitchen when you leave us, will you go into the bathroom for a while, and look at the mirror?"

Donald consented. His friend, John, arrived. He was a magnificent man physically, but in his face there was a strange quality of decadence, a laxity about the eyes and mouth, something on the verge of perverseness, which fascinated Dorothy. It was as if none of the ordinary pleasures of love could satisfy him. In his face there was a peculiar insatiability, curiosity—he had something of the animal. His lips bared his teeth. He seemed startled at the sight of Dorothy.

"I like women of fine breed," he said immediately and looked gratefully at Donald for the gift, the surprise of her presence.

Dorothy was all in fur from head to toe—hat, muff, gloves, even fur on her shoes. Her perfume had already filled the room.

John stood above her, smiling. His gestures were growing more festive. Suddenly he bent forward like some stage director and said: "I have something to ask you. You are so beautiful. I hate the clothes which conceal a woman. Yet I hate to take them off. Will you do something for me, something exceptionally wonderful? Please take your clothes off in the other room and come back here in only your furs. Will you? I'll tell you why I ask you this. Only thoroughbred women look beautiful in furs, and you are a thoroughbred."

Dorothy went into the bathroom, slipped out of her clothes and returned in her furs, keeping on only her stockings and little fur-trimmed shoes.

John's eyes glittered with pleasure. He could only sit and look at her. His excitement was so strong and contagious that Dorothy began to feel her breasts growing sensitive at the tips. She had a feeling that she wanted to expose them, that she wanted to open the fur and watch John's pleasure. Usually the warmth and stirring of the nipples occurred together with the warmth and stirring of the sex mouth. Today she could feel only her breasts, the compulsion to expose them, to raise them with her hands, to offer them. John leaned over and put his mouth to them.

Donald had left. He waited in the bathroom and looked into the mirror of the door. He saw Dorothy standing by John, her breasts in her hands. The fur had opened to reveal her whole body, glowing, luminous, rich in the fur, like some jeweled animal. Donald was stirred. John did not touch the body, he suckled at the breasts, sometimes stopping to feel the fur with his mouth, as if he were kissing a beautiful animal. The odor of her sex—pungent shell and sea odors, as if woman came out of the sea as Venus did—mixed with the odor of the fur, and John's suckling grew more violent. Seeing Dorothy in the mirror, seeing the hair of her sex like the hair of the fur, Donald felt that if John touched her between the legs he would strike him. He came out of the bathroom, his penis exposed and erect, and walked towards Dorothy. This was so much like the first scene of her passion for Robert that she moaned with joy, tore herself from John and turned fully upon Donald, saying: "Take me, take me!"

Closing her eyes, she imagined Robert crouching over her, tigerlike, tearing open the fur, and caressing her with many hands and mouths and tongues, touching every part of her, parting her legs, kissing her, biting her, licking her. She incited the two men to a frenzy. Nothing was heard but the breathing, the little suckling sounds, the sound of the penis swimming in her moisture.

Leaving them both drowsy, she dressed and went so quickly that they barely were aware of it. Donald cursed: "She couldn't wait. She couldn't wait, she had to go back to him just as before. All wet and juicy from other men's love-making."

It was true that Dorothy did not wash. When Robert arrived home a few moments after her, she was filled with rich odors, open, vibrating still. Her eyes, her gestures, her languid pose on the couch invited him. Robert knew her moods. He was quick to respond to them. He was so happy that she was as she had been long ago. She would be moist between the legs now, responsive. He plunged into her.

Robert was never quite certain of when she was coming. The penis is rarely aware of this spasm in woman, this little palpitation. The penis can feel only its own ejaculation. This time Robert wanted to feel the spasm in Dorothy, the wild little clutching. He withheld his orgasm. She was convulsed. The moment seemed to have come. He forgot his watching in his own wave of pleasure. And Dorothy carried off her deception, unable to reach the orgasm that she had had only an hour before while closing her eyes and pretending it was Robert who was taking her.

Sirocco

Whenever I went down to the beach in Deya I saw two young women, one small and boyish, with short hair and a round, humorous face; the other, like a Viking, with a regal head and body.

They kept to themselves during the day. Strangers always spoke to one another in Deya because there was only one food shop, and everyone met at the small post office. But the two women never spoke to anyone. The tall one was beautiful, with heavy eyebrows, thick dark hair, and light-blue eyes densely fringed. I always looked at her with wonder.

Their secrecy troubled me. They were not joyous. They lived a sort of hypnotic life. They swam quietly, lay on the sand reading.

Then came the sirocco from Africa. It lasts for several days. Not only is it hot and dry, but it travels in a series of whirlwinds, turning feverishly, encircling one, beating one, battering doors, breaking shutters, sending fine dust into the eyes, into the throat, drying everything and irritating the nerves. One cannot sleep, cannot walk, cannot sit still, cannot read. The mind is set whirling exactly like the wind.

The wind is charged with perfumes from Africa, heavy sensual animal odors. It gives a kind of fever and turmoil of the nerves.

One afternoon I had been caught by it while I still had a half-hour's walk to my house. The two women were walking ahead of me, holding on to their skirts, which the wind tried to raise around their heads. As I passed their house they saw me struggling against the dust and blinding heat and said, "Come in and wait until it calms down."

We went in together. They lived in a Moorish tower that they had bought for very little money. The old doors did not close well, and the wind opened them over and over again. I sat with them in a big circular stone room with peasant furniture.

The younger woman left us to make tea. I sat with the Viking princess, whose face was flushed by the fever of the sirocco. She said, "This wind will drive me crazy if it does not stop." She got up several times to close the door. It was exactly as though some intruder wanted to enter the room and was each time repulsed, only to succeed again in opening the door. The woman must have felt this, for she repulsed the intrusion with anger and a growing fear.

What the wind seemed to be pushing into the tower room, the Viking knew she could not keep out altogether; for she began to talk.

She spoke as though she were in a confessional, in a dark Catholic confessional, with her eyes lowered, trying not to see the face of the priest, and seeking to be truthful and to remember everything.

"I thought I could find peace here, but since this wind has started it is as though it has stirred everything that I want to forget.

"I was born in one of the most uninteresting of western towns in America. I spent my days reading about foreign countries and was determined to live abroad at all cost. I was in love with my husband even before I met him because I had heard that he lived in China. When he fell in love with me, I expected it, as if it had all been planned beforehand. I was marrying China. I could barely see him as an ordinary man. He was tall, lean, about thirty-five, but he looked older. His life in China had been hard. He was vague about his occupations—he had worked at many things to earn money. He wore glasses and looked like a student. Somehow I was in love with the idea of China, so much that it seemed to me that my husband was no longer a white man but an Oriental. I thought he smelled different from other men.

"We soon went to China. When I arrived there I found a lovely, delicate house full of servants. That the women were exceptionally beautiful did not seem strange to me. That is how I had pictured them. They waited on me slavishly, adoringly, I thought. They brushed my hair, taught me to arrange flowers, to sing and write and speak their language.

"We slept in separate rooms but the partitions were like

cardboard. The beds were hard, low, with thin mattresses, so that at first I did not sleep well at all.

"My husband would stay a little while with me and then leave me. I began to notice sounds that came from the next room, like the wrestling of bodies. I could hear the rustle of the mats, occasionally a stifled murmur. At first I did not realize what it was. I got up noiselessly and opened the door. I saw then that my husband was lying there with two or three of the servant girls, caressing them. In the semidarkness their bodies were completely entangled. When I came in he chased them away. I wept.

"My husband said to me, 'I have lived so long in China I am used to them. I married you because I fell in love with you, but I cannot enjoy you as I do the other women . . . and I can't tell you why.'

"But I pleaded with him to tell me the truth, pleaded and begged him. After a moment he said, 'They are so small sexually, and you are larger . . .'

"'What will I do now?' I said. 'Are you going to send me home? I can't live here with you making love to other women in the room next to mine.'

"He tried to console me, comfort me. He even caressed me, but I turned away and fell asleep weeping.

"The next evening, when I was in bed he came over to me and said, smiling, 'If you say you love me, and you don't really want to leave me, then will you let me try something that may help us enjoy each other?'

"I was so desperate and so jealous that I promised I would do anything he asked of me.

"Then my husband undressed himself and I saw that his penis was covered by a contraption made of rubber and covered with small rubber spikes. It made his penis enormous. It frightened me. But I let him take me this way. It hurt at first, although the spikes were made of rubber, but when I saw that he was enjoying it, I let him continue. All my concern now was whether this pleasure would make him faithful to me. He swore to me that it would, that he no longer wanted his Chinese women. But I would lie awake at night listening for the sounds in his room.

"Once or twice I am sure I heard them, but I did not have the courage to make certain. I became obsessed with the idea that my sex was growing larger and that I would give him less pleasure. Finally I reached such a state of anxiety that I grew ill, began to lose my beauty. I decided to run away from him. I went to Shanghai and stayed in a hotel. I had wired my parents for money so I could sail for home.

"At the hotel I met an American writer, a tall man, heavy, tremendously dynamic, who treated me as if I were a man, a companion. We went out together. He slapped my back when he was happy. We drank and explored Shanghai.

"Once he got drunk in my room and we began to wrestle together like two men. He spared me no tricks. We lay in all kinds of poses, twisting each other around. He got me on the floor with my legs around his neck, then on the bed with my head thrown back touching the floor. I thought my back would break. I loved his strength and weight. I could smell his body as we pressed against each other. We panted. I struck my head against the leg of a chair. We wrestled for such a long time.

"When I was with my husband I had been made to feel ashamed of my height, strength. This man called it all out and enjoyed it. I felt free. He said, 'You are like a tigress. I love that.'

"When we ended our wrestling we were both exhausted. We fell on the bed. My slacks were torn, the belt was broken. My shirt was hanging out. We laughed together. He took another drink. I lay back panting. Then he buried his head under my shirt and began kissing my belly and pulling down my slacks.

"Suddenly the telephone rang and made me jump. Who could that be? I knew no one in Shanghai. I took the receiver; it was my husband's voice. Somehow he had found out where I was. He was talking, talking. Meanwhile my friend had recovered from the surprise of the telephone call and was continuing his caresses. I felt such pleasure talking with my husband and listening to his pleadings to return home . . . and all this while my drunken friend took every liberty with me, having succeeded in pulling down my slacks, biting me between the legs, taking advantage of my position on the bed, kissing me, fondling my breasts. The pleasure was so acute that I delayed the conversation. I discussed everything with my husband. He was promising to send away the servant girls, he wanted to come to the hotel.

"I remembered all he had done to me, in the room next to mine, his callousness in deceiving me. I was taken with a diabolical impulse. I said to my husband, 'Don't try to come and see me. I am living with somebody else. In fact he is lying here and caressing me while I talk to you.'

"I heard my husband curse me in the foulest words he could muster. I was happy. I hung up the receiver and sank under the big body of my new friend.

"I began traveling with him. . . ."

The sirocco had again blown the door open, and the woman went to close it. The wind was dying now, and this was the last of its violence. The woman sat down. I thought that she would go on. I was curious about her young companion. But she remained silent. After a while I left. The next day when we met at the post office she did not even seem to recognize me.

The Maja

The painter Novalis was newly married to María, a Spanish woman with whom he had fallen in love because she resembled the painting he most loved, the *Maja Desnuda*, by Goya.

They went to live in Rome. María clapped her hands in childish joy when she saw the bedroom, admiring the sumptuous Venetian furniture with its wonderful inlaid pearl and ebony.

That first night María, lying on the monumental bed made for the wife of a doge, trembled with delight, stretching her limbs before she hid them under the fine sheets. The pink toes of her plump little feet moved as if they were calling Novalis.

But not once had she shown herself completely nude to her husband. First of all she was Spanish, then Catholic, then thoroughly bourgeois. Before lovemaking the light had to be put out.

Standing beside the bed, Novalis looked at her with his brows contracted, dominated by a desire that he hesitated to express; he wanted to see her, to admire her. He did not fully know her yet despite those nights in the hotel when they could hear strange voices on the other side of the thin walls. What he asked was not the caprice of a lover, but the desire of a painter, of an artist. His eyes were hungry for her beauty.

María resisted, blushing, a trifle angry, her deepest prejudices offended.

"Don't be foolish, Novalis, dearest," she said. "Come to bed."

But he persisted. She must overcome her bourgeois scruples, he said. Art scoffed at such modesty, human beauty was meant to be shown in all its majesty and not to be kept hidden, despised.

His hands, restrained by the fear of hurting her, gently pulled her weak arms, which were crossed on her breast.

She laughed. "You silly thing. You're tickling me. You're hurting me."

But little by little, her feminine pride flattered by this worship of her body, she gave in to him, allowed herself to be treated like a child, with soft remonstrances, as if she were undergoing a pleasant torture.

Her body, freed from veils, shone with the whiteness of pearl. María closed her eyes as if she wanted to flee from the shame of her nakedness. On the smooth sheet, her graceful form intoxicated the eyes of the artist.

"You are Goya's fascinating little maja," he said.

In the weeks that followed she would neither pose for him nor allow him to use models. She would appear unexpectedly in his studio and chat with him while he painted. One afternoon when she came suddenly into the studio she saw on the model's platform a naked woman lying in some furs, showing the curves of her ivory back.

Later María made a scene. Novalis begged her to pose for him; she capitulated. Tired out by the heat, she fell asleep. He worked for three hours without a pause.

With frank immodesty, she admired herself in the canvas just as she did in the great mirror in the bedroom. Dazzled by the beauty of her own body, she momentarily lost her self-consciousness. Also, Novalis had painted a different face on her body so that no one would recognize her.

But afterwards, María fell again into her old habits of thinking, refused to pose. She made a scene each time Novalis engaged a model, watching and listening behind doors and quarreling constantly.

She became quite ill with anxiety and morbid fears and developed insomnia. The doctor gave her pills which sent her off into a deep sleep.

Novalis noticed that when she took these pills she did not hear him get up, move about, or even spill objects in the room. One morning he awakened early, with the intention of working, and watched her sleep, so deeply that she rarely stirred at all. A strange idea occurred to him.

He drew back the sheets that covered her, and slowly began to lift up her silk nightgown. He was able to raise it above her breasts without her giving any sign of awakening.

Now her whole body lay exposed and he could contemplate it as long as he wanted. Her arms were flung outwards; her breasts lay under his eyes like an offering. He was roused with desire for her but still did not dare touch her. Instead he brought his drawing paper and pencils, sat at her side and sketched her. As he worked, he had the feeling that he was caressing each perfect line in her body.

He was able to continue for two hours. When he observed the effect of the sleeping pills beginning to wear off, he pulled down the nightgown, covered her with the sheet and left the room.

Later, María was surprised to notice a new enthusiasm for work in her husband. He locked himself in his studio for whole days, painting from the pencil sketches he made in the mornings.

In this way he completed several paintings of her, always reclining, always asleep, as she had been the first day she posed. María was amazed by this obsession. She thought it was merely a repetition of the first pose. He always altered the face. Since her actual expression was forbidding and severe, no one who saw these paintings ever imagined that the voluptuous body was that of María.

Novalis no longer desired his wife when she was awake, with her puritanical expression and stern eyes. He desired her when she was asleep, abandoned, rich and soft.

He painted her without respite. When he was alone with a new painting in his studio he lay on the couch in front of it, and then a warmth ran through his whole body, as his eyes rested on the maja's breasts, on the valley of her belly, on the hair between her legs. He began to feel an erection stirring. He was surprised at the violent effect of the painting.

One morning he stood in front of María as she lay sleeping. He had succeeded in parting her legs slightly, so as to see the line between them. Watching her unconstrained pose, her opened legs, he fingered his sex with the illusion that she was doing it. How often he had led her hand to his penis, trying to obtain this caress from her, but she was always repulsed and moved her hand away. Now he enclosed his penis fully in his own strong hand.

María soon realized that she had lost his love. She did not know how to win it back. She became aware that he was in love with her body only as he painted it.

She went to the country to stay with friends for a week. But after a few days she fell ill and returned home to see her doctor. When she arrived at the house it looked uninhabited. She tiptoed to Novalis's studio. There was no sound. Then she began to imagine that he was making love to a woman. She approached the door. Slowly and noiselessly, like a thief, she opened it. And this is what she saw: on the floor of the studio, a painting of herself; and lying over it, rubbing himself against it, her husband, naked, with his hair wild, as she had never seen him, his penis erect.

He moved against the painting lasciviously, kissing it, fondling it between the legs. He lay against it as he never had against her. He seemed driven into a frenzy, and all around him were the other paintings of her, nude, voluptuous, beautiful. He threw a passionate glance at them and continued his imaginary embrace. It was an orgy with her he was having, with a wife he had not known in reality. At the sight of this, María's own controlled sensuality flared up, free for the first time. When she took off her clothes, she revealed a María new to him, a María illumined with passion, abandoned as in the paintings, offering her body shamelessly, without hesitation to all his embraces, striving to efface the paintings from his emotions, to surpass them.

A Model

My mother had European ideas about young girls. I was sixteen. I had never gone out alone with young men, I had never read anything but literary novels, and by choice I never was like girls of my age. I was what you would call a sheltered person, very much like some Chinese woman, instructed in the art of making the most of the discarded dresses sent to me by a rich cousin, singing and dancing, writing elegantly, reading the finest books, conversing intelligently, arranging my hair beautifully, keeping my hands white and delicate, using only the refined English I had learned since my arrival from France, dealing with everybody in terms of great politeness.

This was what was left of my European education. But I was very much like the Orientals in one other way: long periods of gentleness were followed by bursts of violence, taking the form of temper and rebellion or of quick decisions and positive action.

I suddenly decided to go to work, without consulting anybody or asking anybody's approval. I knew my mother would be against my plan.

I had rarely gone to New York alone. Now I walked the streets, answering all kinds of advertisements. My accomplishments were not very practical. I knew languages but not typewriting. I knew Spanish dancing but not the new ballroom dances. Everywhere I went I did not inspire confidence. I looked even younger than my age and over-delicate, over-sensitive. I looked as if I could not bear any burdens put on me, yet this was only an appearance.

After a week I had obtained nothing but a sense of not being useful to anyone. It was then I went to see a family friend who was very fond of me. She had disapproved of my mother's way of protecting me. She was happy to see me, amazed at my decision and willing to help me. It was while talking to her humorously about myself, enumerating my assets, that I happened to say that a painter had come to see us the week before and had said that I had an exotic face. My friend jumped up.

"I have it," she said. "I know what you can do. It is true that you have an unusual face. Now I know an art club where the artists go for their models. I will introduce you there. It is a sort of protection for the girls, instead of having them walk about from studio to studio. The artists are registered at the club, where they are known, and they telephone when they need a model."

When we arrived at the club on Fifty-seventh Street, there was great animation and many people. It turned out that they were preparing for the annual show. Every year all the models were dressed in costumes that best suited them and exhibited to the painters. I was quickly registered for a small fee and was sent upstairs to two elderly ladies who took me into the costume room. One of them chose an eighteenth-century costume. The other fixed my hair above my ears. They taught me how to wax my eyelashes. I saw a new self in the mirrors. The rehearsal was going on. I had to walk downstairs and stroll all around the room. It was not difficult. It was like a masquerade ball.

The day of the show everyone was rather nervous. Much of a model's success depended on this event. My hand trembled as I made up my eyelashes. I was given a rose to carry, which made me feel a little ridiculous. I was received with applause. After all the girls had walked slowly around the room, the painters talked with us, took down our names, made engagements. My engagement book was filled like a dance card.

Monday at nine o'clock I was to be at the studio of a well-known painter; at one, at the studio of an illustrator; at four o'clock, at the studio of a miniaturist, and so on. There were women painters too. They objected to our using make-up. They said that when they engaged a made-up model and then got her to wash her face before posing, she did not look the same. For that reason posing for women did not attract us very much.

My announcement at home that I was a model came like a thunderbolt. But it was done. I could make twenty-five dollars a week. My mother wept a little, but was pleased deep down.

That night we talked in the dark. Her room connected with mine and the door was open. My mother was worrying about what I knew (or did not know) about sex.

The sum of my knowledge was this: that I had been kissed many times by Stephen, lying on the sand at the beach. He had been lying over me, and I had felt something bulky and hard pressing against me, but that was all, and to my great amazement when I came home I had discovered that I was all wet between the legs. I had not mentioned this to my mother. My private impression was that I was a great sensualist, that this getting wet between the legs at being kissed showed dangerous tendencies for the future. In fact, I felt quite like a whore.

My mother asked me, "Do you know what happens when a man takes a woman?"

"No," I said, "but I would like to know *how* a man takes a woman in the first place."

"Well, you know the small penis you saw when you bathed your brother—that gets big and hard and the man pushes it inside of the woman."

That seemed ugly to me. "It must be difficult to get it in," I said.

"No, because the woman gets wet before that, so it slides in easily."

Now I understood the mystery of the wetness.

In that case, I thought to myself, I will never get raped, because to get wet you have to like the man.

A few months before, having been violently kissed in the woods by a big Russian who was bringing me home from a dance, I had come home and announced that I was pregnant.

Now I remembered how one night when several of us were returning from another dance, driving along the speedway, we had heard girls screaming. My escort, John, stopped the car. Two girls ran to us from the bushes, disheveled, dresses torn, and eyes haggard. We let them into the car. They were mumbling chaotically about having been taken for a ride on a motorcycle and then attacked. One of them kept saying: "If he broke through, I'll kill myself."

John stopped at an inn and I took the girls to the ladies' room. They immediately went in to the toilet together. One was saying: "There is no blood. I guess he didn't break through." The other one was crying.

We took them home. One of the girls thanked me and said, "I hope that never happens to you."

While my mother was talking I was wondering if she feared this and was preparing me.

I cannot say that when Monday came I was not uneasy. I felt that if the painter was attractive I would be in greater danger than if he was not, for if I liked him I might get wet between the legs.

The first one was about fifty, bald, with a rather European face and little mustache. He had a beautiful studio.

He placed the screen in front of me so that I could change my dress. I threw my clothes over the screen. As I threw my last piece of underwear over the top of the screen I saw the painter's face appear at the top, smiling. But it was done so comically and ridiculously, like a scene in a play, that I said nothing, got dressed, and took the pose.

Every half-hour I would get a rest. I could smoke a cigarette. The painter put on a record and said: "Will you dance?"

We danced on the highly polished floor, turning among the paintings of beautiful women. At the end of the dance, he kissed my neck. "So dainty," he said. "Do you pose in the nude?"

"No."

"Too bad."

I thought this was not so difficult to manage. It was time to pose again. The three hours passed quickly. He talked while he worked. He said he had married his first model; that she was unbearably jealous; that every now and then she broke into the studio and made scenes; that she would not let him paint from the nude. He had rented another studio she did not know about. Often he worked there. He gave parties there too. Would I like to come to one on Saturday night?

He gave me another little kiss on the neck as I left. He winked and said: "You won't tell the club on me?"

I returned to the club for luncheon because I could make up my face and freshen myself, and they gave us a cheap lunch. The other girls were there. We fell into conversation. When I mentioned the invitation for Saturday night, they laughed, nodding at one another. I could not get them to talk. One girl had lifted up her skirt and was examining a mole way up her thighs. With a little caustic pencil she was trying to burn it away. I saw that she was not wearing panties, just a black satin dress which clung to her. The telephone would ring and then one of the girls would be called and go off to work.

The next was a young illustrator. He was wearing his shirt open at the neck. He did not move when I came in. He shouted at me, "I want to see a lot of back and shoulders. Put a shawl around yourself or something." Then he gave me a small old-fashioned umbrella and white gloves. The shawl he pinned down almost to my waist. This was for a magazine cover.

The arrangement of the shawl over my breasts was precarious. As I tilted my head at the angle he wanted, in a sort of inviting gesture, the shawl slipped and my breasts showed. He would not let me move. "Wish I could paint them in," he said.

He was smiling as he worked with his charcoal pencil. Leaning over to measure me, he touched the tips of my breasts with his pencil and made a little black mark. "Keep that pose," he said as he saw me ready to move. I kept it.

Then he said: "You girls sometimes act as if you thought you were the only ones with breasts or asses. I see so many of them they don't interest me, I assure you. I take my wife all dressed always. The more clothes she has on the better. I turn off the light. I know too much how women are made. I've drawn millions of them."

The little touch of the pencil on my breasts had hardened the tips. This angered me, because I had not felt it a pleasure at all. Why were my breasts so sensitive, and did he notice it?

He went on drawing and coloring his picture. He stopped to drink a whiskey and offered me some. He dipped his finger in the whiskey and touched one of my nipples. I was not posing so I moved away angrily. He kept smiling at me. "Doesn't it feel nice?" he said. "It warms them."

It was true that the tips were hard and red.

"Very nice nipples you have. You don't need to use lipstick on them, do you? They are naturally rosy. Most of them have a leather color."

I covered myself.

That was all for that day. He asked me to come the next day at the same time.

He was slower in getting to his work on Tuesday. He talked. He had his feet up on his drawing table. He offered me a cigarette. I was pinning up my shawl. He was watching me. He said: "Show me your legs. I may do a drawing of legs next time."

I lifted up my skirt above the knee.

"Sit down with your skirt up high," he said.

He sketched in the legs. There was a silence.

Then he got up, flung his pencil on the table, leaned over

me and kissed me fully on the mouth, forcing my head backwards. I pushed him off violently. This made him smile. He slipped his hand swiftly up under my skirt, felt my thighs where the stockings stopped and before I could move was back in his seat.

I took the pose and said nothing, because I had just made a discovery—that in spite of my anger, in spite of the fact that I was not in love, the kiss and the caress on the naked thighs had given me pleasure. While I fought him off, it was only out of a habit, but actually it had given me pleasure.

The pose gave me time to awaken from the pleasure and remember my defenses. But my defenses had been convincing and he was quiet for the rest of the morning.

From the very first I had divined that what I really had to defend myself against was my own susceptibility to caresses. I was also filled with great curiosities about so many things. At the same time I was utterly convinced that I would not give myself to anyone but the man I fell in love with.

I was in love with Stephen. I wanted to go to him and say: "Take me, take me!" I suddenly remembered another incident, and that was a year before this when one of my aunts had taken me to New Orleans to the Mardi Gras. Friends of hers had driven us in their automobile. There were two other young girls with us. A band of young men took advantage of the confusion, the noise, the excitement and gaiety to jump into our automobile, remove our masks and begin kissing us while my aunt raised an outcry. Then they disappeared into the crowd. I was left dazed and wishing that the young man who had taken hold of me and had kissed me on the mouth were still there. I was languid from the kiss, languid and stirred.

Back at the club I wondered what all the rest of the models felt. There was a great deal of talk about defending oneself, and I wondered whether it was all sincere. One of the loveliest models, whose face was not particularly beautiful but who had a magnificent body, was talking:

"I don't know what other girls feel about posing in the nude," she said, "I love it. Ever since I was a little girl I liked taking off my clothes. I liked to see how people looked at me. I used to take off my clothes at parties, as soon as people were a little drunk. I liked showing my body. Now I can't wait to take them off. I enjoy being looked at. It gives me pleasure. I get shivers of pleasure right down my back when men look at me. And when I pose for a whole class of artists at the school, when I see all those eyes on my body, I get so much pleasure, it is—well, it is like being made love to. I feel beautiful, I feel as women must feel sometimes when undressed for a lover. I enjoy my own body. I like to pose holding my breasts in my hand. Sometimes I caress them. I was once in burlesque. I loved it. I enjoyed doing that as much as the men enjoyed seeing it. The satin of the dress used to give me shivers—taking my breasts out, exposing myself. That excited me. When men touched me I did not get as much excitement . . . it was always a disappointment. But I know other girls who don't feel that way."

"I feel humiliated," said a red-haired model. "I feel my body is not my own, and that it no longer has any value . . . being seen by everybody."

"I don't feel anything at all," said another. "I feel it's all impersonal. When men are painting or drawing, they no longer think of us as human beings. One painter told me that the body of a model on the stand is an objective thing, that the only moment he felt disturbed erotically was when the model took off her kimono. In Paris, they tell me, the model undresses right in front of the class, and that's exciting."

"If it were all so objective," said another girl, "they wouldn't invite us to parties afterwards."

"Or marry their models," I added, remembering two

painters I had already met who had married their favorite models.

One day I had to pose for an illustrator of stories. When I arrived I found two other people already there, a girl and man. We were to compose scenes together, love scenes for a romance. The man was about forty, with a very mature, very decadent face. It was he who knew how to arrange us. He placed me in position for a kiss. We had to hold the pose while the illustrator photographed us. I was uneasy. I did not like the man at all. The other girl played the jealous wife who burst in upon the scene. We had to do it many times. Each time the man acted the kiss I shrank inside of myself, and he felt it. He was offended. His eyes were mocking. I acted badly. The illustrator was shouting at me as if we were taking a moving picture, "More passion, put more passion into it!"

I tried to remember how the Russian had kissed me on returning from the dance, and that relaxed me. The man repeated the kiss. And now I felt he was holding me closer than he needed to, and surely he did not need to push his tongue into my mouth. He did it so quickly that I had no time to move. The illustrator started other scenes.

The male model said, "I have been a model for ten years now. I don't know why they always want young girls. Young girls have no experience and no expression. In Europe young girls of your age, under twenty, do not interest anyone. They are left in school or at home. They only become interesting after marriage."

As he talked I thought of Stephen. I thought of us at the beach, lying on the hot sand. I knew that Stephen loved me. I wanted him to take me. I wanted now to be made a woman quickly. I did not like being a virgin, always defending myself. I felt that everyone knew I was a virgin and was all the more keen to conquer me.

That evening Stephen and I were going out together. Somehow or other I must tell him. I must tell him that I was in danger of being raped, that he'd better do it first. No, he would then be so anxious. How could I tell him?

I had news for him. I was the star model now. I had more work than anyone in the club, there were more demands for me because I was a foreigner and had an unusual face. I often had to pose in the evenings. I told Stephen all this. He was proud of me.

"You like your posing?" he said.

"I love it. I love to be with painters, to see them work—good or bad, I like the atmosphere of it, the stories I hear. It is varied, never the same. It is really adventure."

"Do they . . . do they make love to you?" Stephen asked.

"Not if you don't want them to."

"But do they try . . . ?"

I saw that he was anxious. We were walking to my house from the railway station, through the dark fields. I turned to him and offered my mouth. He kissed me. I said, "Stephen, take me, take me, take me."

He was completely dumbfounded. I was throwing myself into the refuge of his big arms, I wanted to be taken and have it all over with, I wanted to be made woman. But he was absolutely still, frightened. He said, "I want to marry you, but I can't do it just now."

"I don't care about the marriage."

But now I became conscious of his surprise, and it quieted me. I was immensely disappointed by his conventional attitude. The moment passed. He thought it was merely an attack of blind passion, that I had lost my head. He was even proud to have protected me against my own impulses. I went home to bed and sobbed.

One illustrator asked me if I would pose on Sunday, that he was in a great rush to finish a poster. I consented. When I arrived he was already at work. It was morning and the building seemed deserted. His studio was on the thirteenth floor. He had half of the poster done. I got undressed quickly and put on the evening dress he had given me to wear. He did not seem to pay any attention to me. We worked in peace for a long while. I grew tired. He noticed it and gave me a rest. I walked about the studio looking at the other pictures. They were mostly portraits of actresses. I asked him who they were. He answered me with details about their sexual tastes:

"Oh, this one, this one demands romanticism. It's the only way you can get near her. She makes it difficult. She is European and she likes an intricate courtship. Halfway through I gave it up. It was too strenuous. She was very beautiful though, and there is something wonderful about getting a woman like that in bed. She had beautiful eyes, an entranced air, like some Hindu mystic. It makes you wonder how they will behave in bed.

"I have known other sexual angels. It is wonderful to see the change in them. These clear eyes that you can see through, these bodies that take such beautiful harmonious poses, these delicate hands . . . how they change when desire takes hold of them. The sexual angels! They are wonderful because it is such a surprise, such a change. You, for instance, with your appearance of never having been touched, I can see you biting and scratching . . . I am sure your very voice changes—I have seen such changes. There are women's voices that sound like poetic, unearthly echoes. Then they change. The eyes change. I believe that all these legends about people changing into animals at night—like the stories of the werewolf, for instance—were invented by men who saw women transform at night from idealized, worshipful creatures into animals and thought that they were possessed. But I know it is something much simpler than that. You are a virgin, aren't you?"

"No, I am married," I said.

"Married or not, you are a virgin. I can tell. I am never deceived. If you are married your husband has not made you a woman yet. Don't you regret that? Don't you feel you are wasting time, that real living only begins with sensation, with being a woman . . . ?"

This corresponded so exactly to what I had been feeling, to my desire to enter experience, that I was silent. I hated to admit this to a stranger.

I was conscious of being alone with the illustrator in an empty studio building. I was sad that Stephen had not understood my desire to become a woman. I was not frightened but fatalistic, desiring only to find someone I might fall in love with.

"I know what you are thinking," he said, "but for me it would not have any meaning unless the woman wanted me. I never could make love to a woman if she did not want me. When I first saw you, I felt how wonderful it would be to initiate you. There is something about you that makes me feel you will have many love affairs. I would like to be the first one. But not unless you wanted it."

I smiled. "That is exactly what I was thinking. It can only be if I want it, and I do not want it."

"You must not give that first surrender so much importance. I think that was created by the people who wanted to preserve their daughters for marriage, the idea that the first man who takes a woman will have complete power over her. I think that is a superstition. It was created to help preserve women from promiscuity. It is actually untrue. If a man can make himself be loved, if he can rouse a woman, then she will be attracted to him. But the mere act of breaking through her virginity is not enough to accomplish this. Any man can do this and leave the woman unaroused. Did you know that many Spaniards take their wives this way and give them many children without completely initiating them sexually just to be sure of their faithfulness? The Spaniard believes in keeping pleasure for his mistress. In fact, if he sees a woman enjoy sensuality, he immediately suspects her of being faithless, even of being a whore."

The illustrator's words haunted me for days. Then I was faced with a new problem. Summer had come and the painters were leaving for the country, for the beach, for far-off places in all directions. I did not have the money to follow them, and I was not sure how much work I would get. One morning I posed for an illustrator named Ronald. Afterwards he set the phonograph going and asked me to dance. While we were dancing he said, "Why don't you come to the country for a while? It will do you good, you will get plenty of work, and I will pay for your trip. There are very few good models there. I am sure you will be kept busy."

So I went. I took a little room in a farmhouse. Then I went to see Ronald, who lived down the road in a shed, into which he had built a huge window. The first thing he did was to blow his cigarette smoke into my mouth. I coughed.

"Oh," he said, "you don't know how to inhale."

"I'm not at all interested," I said, getting up. "What kind of pose do you want?"

"Oh," he said laughing, "we don't work so hard here. You will have to learn to enjoy yourself a little. Now, take the smoke from my mouth and inhale it . . ."

"I don't like to inhale."

He laughed again. He tried to kiss me. I moved away.

"Oh, oh," he said, "you are not going to be a very pleasant companion for me. I paid for your trip, you know, and I'm lonely down here. I expected you to be very pleasant company. Where is your suitcase?"

"I took a room down the road."

"But you were invited to stay with me," he said.

"I understood you wanted me to pose for you."

"For the moment it is not a model I need."

I started to leave. He said, "You know, there is an under-standing here about models who do not know how to enjoy themselves. If you take this attitude nobody will give you any work."

I did not believe him. The next morning I began to knock on the doors of all the artists I could find. But Ronald had already paid them a visit. So I was received without cordiality, like a person who has played a trick on another. I did not have the money to return home, nor the money to pay for my room. I knew nobody. The country was beautiful, moun-tainous, but I could not enjoy it.

The next day I took a long walk and came upon a log cabin by the side of a river. I saw a man painting there, out of doors. I spoke to him. I told him my story. He did not know Ronald, but he was angry. He said he would try to help me. I told him all I wanted was to earn enough to return to New York.

So I began to pose for him. His name was Reynolds. He was a man of thirty or so, with black hair, very soft black eyes and a brilliant smile—a recluse. He never went to the village, except for food, nor frequented the restaurants or bars. He had a lax walk, easy gestures. He had been on the sea, always on tramp steamers, working as a sailor so that he could see foreign countries. He was always restless.

He painted from memory what he had seen in his travels. Now he sat at the foot of a tree and never looked around him but painted a wild piece of South American jungle.

Once when he and his friends were in the jungle, Reyn-olds told me, they had smelled such a strong animal odor they thought they would suddenly see a panther, but out of the bushes had sprung with incredible velocity a woman, a naked savage woman, who looked at them with the frightened eyes of an animal, then ran off, leaving this strong animal scent behind her, threw herself into the river and swam away before they could catch their breath.

A friend of Reynolds had captured a woman like this. When he had washed off the red paint with which she was covered, she was very beautiful. She was gentle when well treated, succumbed to gifts of beads and ornaments.

Her strong smell repelled Reynolds until his friend had offered to let him have a night with her. He had found her black hair as hard and bristly as a beard. The animal smell made him feel he was lying with a panther. And she was so much stronger than he that after a while, he was acting almost like a woman, and she was the one who was molding him to suit her fancies. She was indefatigable and slow to arouse. She could bear caresses that exhausted him, and he fell asleep in her arms.

Then he found her climbing over him and pouring a little liquid over his penis, something that at first made him smart and then aroused him furiously. He was frightened. His penis seemed to have filled with fire, or with red peppers. He rubbed himself against her flesh, more to ease the burning than out of desire.

He was angry. She was smiling and laughing softly. He began taking her with a rage, driven by a fear that what she had done to him would arouse him for the last time, that it was some sort of enchantment to get the maximum of desire from him, until he died.

She lay back laughing, her white teeth showing, the animal odor of her now affecting him erotically like the smell of musk. She moved with such vigor that he felt she would tear his penis away from him. But now he wanted to subjugate her. He caressed her at the same time.

She was surprised by this. No one seemed to have done this to her before. When he was tired of taking her, after two orgasms, he continued to rub her clitoris, and she enjoyed this, begging for more, opening her legs wide. Then suddenly she turned over, crouched on the bed and swung her ass upward at an incredible angle. She expected him to take her again, but he continued to caress her. After this it was always his hand that she sought. She rubbed against it like a huge cat. During the day, if she met him she would rub her sex against his hand, surreptitiously.

Reynolds said that that night had made white women seem weak to him. He was laughing as he told the story.

His painting had reminded him of the savage woman hiding in the bushes, waiting like a tigress to leap and run away from the men who carried guns. He had painted her in, with her heavy, pointed breasts, her fine, long legs, her slender waist.

I did not know how I could pose for him. But he was thinking of another picture. He said, "It will be easy. I want you to fall asleep. But you will be wrapped in white sheets. I saw something in Morocco once that I always wanted to paint. A woman had fallen asleep among her silk spools, holding the silk weaving frame with her hennaed feet. You have beautiful eyes, but they'll have to be closed."

He went into the cabin and brought out sheets which he draped around me like a robe. He propped me against a wooden box, arranged my body and hands as he wanted them and began to sketch immediately. It was a very hot day. The sheets made me warm, and the pose was so lazy that I actually fell asleep, I don't know for how long. I felt languid and unreal. And then I felt a soft hand between my legs, very soft, caressing me so lightly I had to awaken to make sure I had been touched. Reynolds was bending over me, but with such an expression of delighted gentleness that I did not move. His eyes were tender, his mouth half open.

"Only a caress," he said, "just a caress."

I did not move. I had never felt anything like this hand softly, softly caressing the skin between my legs without touching my sex. He only touched the tips of my pubic hair. Then his hand slipped down to the little valley around the sex. I was growing lax and soft. He leaned over and put his mouth on mine, lightly touching my lips, until my own mouth responded, and only then did he touch the tip of my tongue with his. His hand was moving, exploring, but so softly, it was tantalizing. I was wet, and I knew if he moved just a little more he would feel this. The languor spread all through my body. Each time his tongue touched mine I felt as if there were another little tongue inside of me, flicking out, wanting to be touched too. His hand moved only around my sex, and then around my ass, and it was as if he magnetized the blood to follow the movements of his hands. His finger touched the clitoris so gently, then slipped between the lips of the vulva. He felt the wetness. He touched this with delight, kissing me, lying over me now, and I did not move. The warmth, the smells of plants around me, his mouth over mine affected me like a drug.

"Only a caress," he repeated gently, his finger moving around my clitoris until the little mound swelled and hardened. Then I felt as if a seed were bursting in me, a joy that made me palpitate under his fingers. I kissed him with gratitude. He was smiling. He said, "Do you want to caress me?"

I nodded yes, but I did not know what he wanted of me. He unbuttoned his pants and I saw his penis. I took it in my hands. He said, "Press harder." He saw then that I did not know how. He took my hand in his and guided me. The little white foam fell all over my hand. He covered himself. He kissed me with the same grateful kiss I had given him after my pleasure.

He said, "Did you know that a Hindu makes love to his wife ten days before he takes her? For ten days they merely caress and kiss."

The thought of Ronald's behavior angered him all over again—the way he had wronged me in everybody's eyes. I said, "Don't get angry. I am happy he did it, because it made me walk away from the village and come here."

"I loved you as soon as I heard you speak with that accent you have. I felt as if I were traveling again. Your face is so different, your walk, your ways. You remind me of the girl I intended to paint in Fez. I saw her only once, asleep like this. I always dreamed of awakening her as I awakened you."

"And I always dreamed of being awakened with a caress like this," I said.

"If you had been awake I might not have dared."

"You, the adventurer, who lived with a savage woman?"

"I did not really live with the savage woman. That happened to a friend of mine. He was always talking about it, so I always tell it as if it had happened to me. I'm really timid with women. I can knock men down and fight and get drunk, but women intimidate me, even whores. They laugh at me. But this happened exactly as I had always planned it would happen."

"But the tenth day I will be in New York," I said laughing.

"The tenth day I will drive you back, if you have to go back. But meanwhile you are my prisoner."

For ten days we worked out in the open, lying in the sun. The sun would warm my body, as Reynolds waited for me to close my eyes. Sometimes I pretended I wanted him to do more to me. I thought that if I closed my eyes he would take me. I liked the way he would walk up to me, like a hunter, making no sound and lying at my side. Sometimes he lifted my dress first and looked at me for a long time. Then he would touch me lightly, as if he did not want to awaken me, until the moisture came. His fingers would quicken. We kept our mouths together, our tongues caressing. I learned to take his penis in my mouth. This excited him terribly. He would lose all his gentleness, push his penis into my mouth, and I was afraid of choking. Once I bit him, hurt him, but he did not mind. I swallowed the white foam. When he kissed me, our faces were covered with it. The marvelous smell of sex impregnated my fingers. I did not want to wash my hands.

I felt that we shared a magnetic current, but at the same time nothing else bound us together. Reynolds had promised to drive me back to New York. He could not stay in the country much longer. I had to find work.

During the drive back Reynolds stopped the car and we lay on a blanket in the woods, resting. We caressed. He said, "Are you happy?"

"Yes."

"Can you continue to be happy, this way? As we are?"

"Why, Reynolds, what is it?"

"Listen, I love you. You know that, but I can't take you. I did that to a girl once, and she got pregnant and had an abortion. She bled to death. Since then I haven't been able to take a woman. I'm afraid. If that should happen to you, I would kill myself."

I had never thought of things like this. I was silent. We kissed for a long time. For the first time he kissed me between the legs instead of caressing me, kissed me until I felt the orgasm. We were happy. He said, "This little wound women have . . . it frightens me."

In New York it was hot and all the artists were still away. I found myself without work. I took up modeling in dress shops. I could easily get work, but when they asked me to go

out in the evenings with the buyers I would refuse and lose
the job. Finally I was taken into a big place near Thirty-
fourth Street where they employed six models. This place was
frightening and gray. There were long rows of clothes and a
few benches for us to sit on. We waited in our slips, to be
ready for quick changes. When our numbers were called, we
helped one another dress.

The three men who sold the dress designs often tried to
fondle us, squeeze us. We took turns staying during the lunch
hour. My greatest fear was that I would be left alone with the
man who was most persistent.

Once when Stephen telephoned to ask if he would see me
that evening, the man came up behind me and put his hand
into my slip to feel my breasts. Not knowing what else to do, I
kicked him while I held the phone and tried to go on talking
to Stephen. He was not discouraged. Next, he tried to feel my
ass. I kicked again.

Stephen was saying, "What is it, what are you saying?"

I ended the conversation and turned on the man. He was
gone.

The buyers admired our physical qualities as much as the
dresses. The head salesman was very proud of me and would
often say, with his hand on my hair, "She's an artist's model."

This made me long to return to posing. I did not want
Reynolds or Stephen to find me here in an ugly office building, wearing dresses for ugly salesmen and buyers.

Finally I was called to model at the studio of a South American painter. He had the face of a woman, pale with big black
eyes, long black hair, and his gestures were languid and
effete. His studio was beautiful—luxuriant rugs, large paintings of nude women, silk hangings; and there was incense
burning. He said he had a very intricate pose to do. He was
painting a big horse running away with a naked woman. He

asked if I had ever ridden on horseback. I said that I had, when I was younger.

"That is marvelous," he said, "exactly what I want. Now, I have made a contraption here which gives me the effect I need."

It was a dummy of a horse without a head, just the body and legs, with a saddle.

He said, "Take your clothes off first, then I will show you. I have difficulty with this part of the pose. The woman is throwing her body back because the horse is running wild, like this." He sat on the dummy horse to show me.

By now I no longer felt timid about posing nude. I took my clothes off and sat on the horse, throwing my body backwards, my arms flying, my legs clasping the horse's flanks so as not to fall. The painter approved. He moved away and looked at me. "It's a hard pose and I do not expect you to keep it very long. Just let me know when you get tired."

He studied me from every side. Then he came up to me and said, "When I made the drawing, this part of the body showed clearly, here, between the legs." He touched me lightly as if it were merely part of his work. I curved in my belly a little to throw the hips forward and then he said, "Now it is fine. Hold it."

He began to sketch. As I sat there I realized that there was one uncommon detail about the saddle. Most saddles, of course, are shaped to follow the contour of the ass and then rise at the pommel, where they are apt to rub against a woman's sex. I had often experienced both the advantages and the disadvantages of being supported there. Once my garter came loose from the stocking and began to dance around inside of my riding trousers. My companions were galloping and I did not want to fall behind, so I continued. The garter, leaping in all directions, finally fell between my sex and the saddle and hurt me. I held on, gritting my teeth.

The pain was strangely mixed with a sensation I could not define. I was a girl then and did not know anything about sex. I thought that a woman's sex was inside of her, and I did not know about the clitoris.

When the ride was over I was in pain. I mentioned what had happened to a girl I knew well and we both went into the bathroom. She helped me out of my trousers, out of my little belt with the garters on it, and then said, "Are you hurt? That's a very sensitive spot. Maybe you'll never have any pleasure there if you got hurt."

I let her look at it. It was red and a little swollen, but not so very painful. What bothered me was her saying I might be deprived of a pleasure by this, a pleasure I did not know. She insisted on bathing it with a wet cotton, fondled me and finally kissed me, "to make it well."

I became acutely aware of this part of my body. Particularly when we rode a long while in the heat, I felt such a warmth and stirring between my legs that all I desired was to get off the horse and let my friend nurse me again. She was always asking me, "Does it hurt?"

So once I answered, "Just a little." We dismounted and went into the bathroom, and she bathed the chafed spot with cotton and cool water.

And again she fondled me, saying, "But it does not look sore anymore. Maybe you will be able to enjoy yourself again."

"I don't know," I said. "Do you think it has gone . . . dead . . . from the pain?"

My friend very tenderly leaned over and touched me. "Does it hurt?"

I lay back and said, "No, I do not feel anything."

"Don't you feel this?" she asked with concern, pressing the lips between her fingers.

"No," I said, watching her.

"Don't you feel this?" She passed her fingers now around the tip of the clitoris, making tiny circles.

"I don't feel anything."

She became eager to see if I had lost my sensibility and increased her caresses, rubbing the clitoris with one hand while she vibrated the tip with the other. She stroked my pubic hair and tender skin around it. Finally I felt her, wildly, and I began to move. She was panting over me, watching me and saying, "Wonderful, wonderful, you can feel there . . ."

I was remembering this as I sat on the dummy horse and noticed that the pommel was quite accentuated. So the painter could see what he wanted to paint, I slid forward, and as I did so my sex rubbed against the leather prominence. The painter was observing me.

"Do you like my horse?" he said. "Do you know that I can make it move?"

"Can you?"

He came near me and set the dummy in motion, and indeed it was perfectly constructed to move like a horse.

"I like it," I said. "It reminds me of the times I rode horseback when I was a girl." I noticed that he stopped painting now to watch me. The motion of the horse pushed my sex against the saddle even harder and gave me great pleasure. I thought that he would notice it, and so I said, "Stop it now." But he smiled and did not stop it. "Don't you like it?" he said.

I did like it. Each movement brought the leather against my clitoris, and I thought I could not hold back an orgasm if it went on. I begged him to stop. My face was flushed.

The painter was carefully watching me, watching every expression of a pleasure I could not control, and now it increased so that I abandoned myself to the motion of the horse, let myself rub against the leather, until I felt the orgasm and I came, riding this way in front of him.

Only then did I know that he expected it, that he had done all this to see me enjoy it. He knew when to stop the machinery. "You can rest now," he said.

Soon after, I went to pose for a woman illustrator, Lena, I had met at a party. She liked company. Actors and actresses came to see her, writers. She painted for magazine covers. The door was always open. People brought drinks. The talk was acid, cruel. It seemed to me that all her friends were caricaturists. Everyone's weaknesses were immediately exposed. Or they exposed their own. One beautiful young man, dressed with great elegance, made no secret of his profession. He sat around at the big hotels, waited for old women who were alone and took them out to dance. Very often they invited him back to their rooms.

Lena made a wry face. "How can you do it?" she asked him. "Such old women, how can you possibly get an erection? If I saw a woman like that lying on my bed, I would run away."

The young man smiled. "There are so many ways of doing it. One is to close my eyes and to imagine it is not an old woman but a woman I like, and then when my eyes are closed I begin to think how pleasant it will be to be able to pay my rent the next day or to buy a new suit or silk shirts. And as I do this, I keep stroking the woman's sex without looking, and, you know, if your eyes are closed, they feel about the same, more or less. Sometimes, though, when I have difficulty I take drugs. Of course, I know that at this rate my career will last about five years and that at the end of that time I will not be of any use even to a young woman. But by then I will be glad never to see a woman again.

"I certainly envy my Argentine friend, my roommate. He is a handsome, aristocratic man, absolutely effete. Women would love him. When I leave the apartment, do you know what he does? He gets up out of bed, pulls out a small electric iron and an ironing board, takes his pants and begins to press them. As he presses them he imagines how he will come out of the building so impeccably dressed, how he will walk down Fifth Avenue, how somewhere he will spy a beautiful woman, follow the scent of her perfume for many blocks, follow her into crowded elevators, almost touching her. The woman will be wearing a veil and a fur around her neck. Her dress will outline her figure.

"After following her thus through the shops, he will finally speak to her. She will see his handsome face smiling at her and the chivalrous way he has of carrying himself. They will go off together and sit having tea somewhere, then go to the hotel where she is staying. She will invite him to come up with her. They will get into the room and then pull down the shades and lie in the darkness making love.

"As he presses his pants carefully, meticulously, my friend imagines how he will make love to this woman—and it excites him. He knows how he will grip her. He likes to push his penis in from behind and raise the woman's legs, and then get her to turn just a little so that he can see it moving in and out. He likes the woman to squeeze the base of his penis at the same time; her fingers press harder than the mouth of her sex, and that excites him. She will also touch his balls as he moves, and he will touch her clitoris, because that gives her a double pleasure. He will make her gasp and shake from head to foot and beg for more.

"By the time he has envisioned all this standing there, half naked, pressing his pants, my friend has a hard on. It is all he wants. He puts away the pants, the iron and the ironing board, and he gets into bed again, lying back and smoking, thinking over this scene until each detail of it is perfect and a drop of semen appears at the head of his penis, which he strokes while he lies smoking and dreaming of pursuing other women.

"I envy him because he can get so much excitement from thinking all this. He questions me. He wants to know how my women are made, how they behave . . ."

Lena laughed. She said, "It's hot. I will take my corset off." And she went into the alcove. When she came back her body looked free and lax. She sat down, crossed her bare legs, her blouse half-open. One of her friends sat where he could see her.

Another one, a handsome man, stood near me as I was posing and whispered compliments. He said, "I love you because you remind me of Europe—Paris especially. I don't know what there is about Paris, but there is sensuality in the air there. It is contagious. It is such a human city. I don't know whether it is because couples are always kissing in the streets, at tables in the cafés, in the movies, in the parks. They embrace each other so freely. They stop for long complete kisses in the middle of the sidewalk, at the subway entrances. Perhaps it is that, or the softness of the air. I don't know. In the dark, in each doorway at night there is a man and woman almost melted into one another. The whores watch for you every moment . . . they touch you.

"One day I was standing on a platform bus, looking up idly at the houses. I saw a window open and a man and woman lying on a bed. The woman was sitting over the man.

"At five o'clock in the afternoon it becomes unbearable. There is love and desire in the air. Everybody is in the streets. The cafés are full. In the movies there are little boxes that are completely dark and curtained off so that you can make love on the floor while the movie is going on and not be seen. It is all so open, so easy. No police to interfere. A woman friend of mine who was followed and annoyed by a man complained to the policeman at the corner. He laughed and said, 'You'll be sorrier the day no man wants to annoy you, won't you? After all, you should be thankful instead of getting angry.' And he would not help her."

Then my admirer said in a lower voice, "Will you come and have dinner with me and go to the theatre?"

He became my first real lover. I forgot Reynolds and Stephen. They now seemed like children to me.

The Queen

The painter sat beside his model mixing colors while he talked about the whores that had stirred him. His shirt was open, showing a strong, smooth neck and a tuft of dark hair; his belt was loosened for comfort, a button was missing from his pants, and his sleeves were turned up for freedom.

He was saying, "I like a whore best of all because I feel

she will never cling to me, never get entangled with me. It makes me feel free. I do not have to make love to her. The only woman who ever gave me the same pleasure was a woman who was incapable of falling in love, who gave herself like a whore, who despised the men she gave herself to. This woman had been a whore and was colder than a statue. The painters had discovered her and used her as a model. She was a magnificent model. She was the very essence of the whore. Somehow in the whore the cold womb, constantly subjected to desire, produces a phenomenon. All the eroticism comes to the surface. The constant living with a penis inside of one does something fascinating to a woman. The womb seems to be exposed, to be present in every aspect of her.

"Somehow or other even the hair of a whore seems impregnated with sex. This woman's hair . . . it was the most sensual hair I have ever seen. Medusa must have had hair like this and with it seduced the men who fell under her spell. It was full of life, heavy, and as pungent as if it had been bathed in sperm. To me it always felt as if it had been wrapped around a penis and soaked in secretions. It was the kind of hair I wanted to wrap around my own sex. It was warm and musky, oily, strong. It was the hair of an animal. It bristled when it was touched. Merely to pass my fingers through it could give me an erection. I would have been content just touching her hair.

"But it was not her hair alone. Her skin was erotic, too. She would lie for hours letting me stroke her, lie like an animal, absolutely quiet, languid . . . The transparence of her skin showed turquoise-blue threads interlacing her body, and I felt that I was not only touching satin but living veins, veins so alive that when I touched her skin I could feel the movement underneath. I used to like lying against her buttocks and caressing her, to feel the contractions of the muscles, which betrayed her responsiveness.

"Her skin was dry like some desert sand. When we first lay in bed it was cool, and then it would become warm and feverish. Her eyes—it is impossible to describe her eyes except by saying that they were the eyes of an orgasm. What constantly happened in her eyes was something so feverish, so incendiary, so intense that at times when I looked straight at her and felt my penis rising and palpitating, I also felt as if something were palpitating in her eyes. With her eyes alone she could give this response, this absolutely erotic response, as if febrile waves were trembling there, pools of madness . . . something devouring that could lick a man all over like a flame, annihilate him, with a pleasure never known before.

"She was the queen of the whores, Bijou. Yes, Bijou. Only a few years ago she could still be seen sitting at some little café in Montmartre, like an Oriental Fatima, but still pale, the eyes still burning. She was like a womb turned inside out. Her mouth, not a mouth that made you think of a kiss, or of food; not a mouth to speak with, to form words, to greet you— no, it was like the mouth of woman's sex itself, the shape of it, the way it moved—to draw you in, to rouse you—always moistened, red and alive like the lips of a caressed sex . . . Each motion of this mouth had the power to awaken the same motion, the same undulation in the sex of a man, as if transmitted by contagion, directly, immediately. As it undulated, like a wave about to curl and engulf one, it ordained the undulation of the penis, the undulation of the blood. As it grew moist, it drew out my erotic secretion.

"Somehow, Bijou's whole body was guided only by eroticism, guided by a genius for exposing every expression of desire. It was indecent, I tell you. It was like making love with her in public, in a café, in the street, before everyone.

"She kept nothing for night, for the bed. It was all in the open, on view. She was indeed the queen of the whores, enacting possession at every instant of her life, even while she ate; and when she played cards, she did not sit impassive, her body deprived of sensuality, as other women would sit with their attention on the game. One felt from the pose of her body, the way her ass spread on the seat, that everything was still set for possession. Her breasts almost touched the table with their fullness. If she laughed, then it was the sexual laugh of a satisfied woman, the laugh of a body enjoying itself through every pore and cell, being caressed by the whole world.

"In the street, walking behind her sometimes when she did not know that I was there, I could see even urchins following her. Before they had seen her face, men followed her. It was as if she left an animal scent behind her. Strange what it can do to a man to see a truly sexual animal before him. The animal nature of woman has been so carefully disguised— the lips and ass and legs made to serve other purposes, made, like some colored plumage, to distract man from his desire rather than accentuate it.

"The women who are unabashedly sexual, with the womb written all over their faces, who arouse in a man the desire to fling his penis at them immediately; the women for whom clothes are only a means of making certain fragments of the body more prominent, like the women who wore bustles to exaggerate their asses, and the women who wore corsets that thrust their breasts out of their clothes; the women who throw their sex out at us, from the hair, the eyes, the nose, the mouth, the whole body—these are the women I love.

"The others . . . how you have to search for the animal in them. They have diluted it, disguised it, perfumed it, so it will smell like something else—like what? angels?

"Let me tell you what happened to me once with Bijou. Bijou was naturally faithless. She asked me to paint her up for the Art Ball. It was a year when the painters and models were supposed to go dressed as African savages. So Bijou asked me to paint her up artistically, and for this purpose she came to my studio a few hours before the ball.

"I set about decorating her body with African designs of my own invention. She stood stark naked before me, and at first I stood up and began to paint her shoulders and breasts, and then I crouched to paint the belly and back, then I kneeled and began to paint the lower part of the body and legs . . . I painted her lovingly, adoringly, like an act of worship.

"Her back was broad, strong, like the back of a circus horse. I could have mounted her and she would not have bent under the burden. I could have sat on this back and slid down and given it to her from behind, like a whip. I wanted to. Even more, perhaps, I wanted to squeeze her breasts until all the paint came off, caressed them clean so that I could kiss them . . . But I restrained myself and continued to paint her into a savage.

"When she moved, the bright designs now moved with her, like an oily sea with undercurrents. Her nipples were hard like berries under the touch of the brush. Every curve gave me a delight. I unfastened my pants. I let my penis free. She never looked at me. She stood there without moving. As I painted the hips and then the valley leading to the pubic hair, she realized I would not be able to finish my task and said, "You will spoil the whole thing if you touch me. You can't touch me. After it is dry, you will be the first. I will wait for you at the ball. But not now." And she smiled at me.

"Of course, the sex remained unpainted. Bijou was going entirely naked but for the semblance of a fig leaf. I was allowed to kiss the unpainted sex—carefully, or I would have swallowed jade green and Chinese red. And Bijou was so proud of her African tattoo designs. Now she looked like the queen of the desert. Her eyes had a hard, lacquered glow. She shook her earrings, laughed, covered herself with a cape and left me. I was in such a state that it took me hours to prepare myself for the ball—merely a coat of brown paint.

"I told you Bijou was a faithless one. She did not even allow the paint to dry. When I arrived I could see that more than one man had braved the dangers of being painted with her own designs. The tattoos were completely blurred. The ball was at its height. The boxes were filled with tangled couples. It was one collective orgasm. And Bijou had not waited for me. As she walked about she left a tiny trail of semen, by which I could have followed her easily anywhere."

Hilda and Rango

Hilda was a beautiful Parisian model who fell deeply in love with an American writer, whose work was so violent and sensual that it attracted women to him immediately. They would write him letters or try for an introduction through his friends. Those who succeeded in meeting him were always amazed by his gentleness, his softness.

Hilda had the same experience. Seeing that he remained impassive, she began to court him. It was only when she had made the first advances, caressed him, that he began making love to her as she had expected to be made love to. But each time, she would have to begin all over. First she had to tempt him in some way—fix a loosened garter, or talk about some experience in the past, or lie on his couch, throw back her head and thrust her breasts forwards, stretching herself like an enormous cat. She would sit on his lap, offer her mouth, unbutton his pants, excite him.

They lived together for several years, deeply attached to each other. She became accustomed to his sexual rhythm. He lay back waiting and enjoying himself. She learned to be active, bold, but she suffered, because she was by nature extraordinarily feminine. Deep down she had the belief that woman could easily control her desire, but that man could not, that it was even harmful for him to try to. She felt that woman was meant to respond to man's desire. She had always dreamed of having a man who would force her will, rule her sexually, lead.

She gratified this man because she loved him. She learned to seek out his penis and touch it until he was aroused, to seek his mouth and stir his tongue, to press her body against his, to incite him. Sometimes they would be lying down and talking. She would place her hand over his penis and find it hard. Yet he made no move towards her. Slowly then, she became used to expressing her own desire, her own moods. She lost all her reserve, her timidity.

One night at a party in Montparnasse, she met a Mexican painter, a huge dark man with heavy charcoal eyes, eyebrows and hair. He was drunk. She was to discover that he was almost always drunk.

But the sight of her gave him a profound shock. He pulled himself up from his faltering, tottering posture and faced her as if he were a big lion facing a tamer. Something about her made him stand still and try to become sober again, to rise from the fog and fumes in which he lived continuously. Something about her face made him stand ashamed of his unkempt clothes, the paint under his nails, the uncombed black hair. She, on the other hand, was struck by this image of a demon, the demon she had imagined to exist behind the work of the American writer.

He was huge, restless, destructive, loved no one, was attached to nothing, a tramp and an adventurer. He would paint at the studios of friends, borrowing oils and canvas, then leave his work there and go off. Most of the time he lived with the gypsies on the outskirts of Paris. With them he shared their life in the gypsy carts, traveling all through France. He respected their laws, never made love to the gypsy women, played the guitar with them at night clubs when they needed money, ate their meals—very often made of stolen chicken.

When he met Hilda he had his own gypsy cart just outside one of the gates of Paris, near the ancient barricades, which were now crumbling. The cart had belonged to a Portuguese who had covered its walls with painted leather. The bed was hung at the back of the cart, suspended like a ship's bunk. The windows were arched. The ceiling was so low it was difficult for one to stand up.

At the party that first evening, Rango did not invite Hilda to dance, although friends of his were providing the music for the night. The lights in the studio had been put out because enough light came from the street, and couples stood on the balcony with their arms around each other. The music was languid and dissolving.

Rango stood above Hilda and stared at her. Then he said, "Do you want to walk?" Hilda said yes. Rango walked with his hands in his pockets, a cigarette dangling from the corner of his mouth. He was sober now, his head as clear as the night. He was walking towards the outskirts of the city. They came to the ragpickers' shacks, little shacks built unevenly, crazily, with sloping roofs and no windows—enough air came through the cracked boards and badly built doors. The paths were made of earth.

A little farther on stood a row of gypsy carts. It was four in the morning, and people were asleep. Hilda did not talk. She walked in the shadow of Rango with a great feeling of being taken out of herself, of having no will and no knowledge of what was happening to her, merely a pervading sense of flow.

Rango's arms were bare. Hilda was aware of only one thing, that she wanted these bare arms to grip her. He bowed to enter his cart. He lit a candle. He was too tall for the low ceiling, but she was smaller and could stand straight.

The candles made huge shadows. His bed was open, merely a blanket thrown back. His clothes were strewn around. There were two guitars. He took one up and began to play, sitting among his clothes. Hilda had the feeling that she was dreaming, that she must keep her eyes on his bare arms, on his throat showing through the open shirt, so that he would feel what she felt, the same magnetism.

At the same moment that she felt she was falling into darkness, into his golden-brown flesh, he fell towards her, covered her with kisses, very hot, quick kisses, into which his breath passed. He kissed her behind her ears, on her eyelids, her throat, her shoulders. She was blinded, deafened, made senseless. Every kiss, like a gulp of wine, added to the warmth of her body. Every kiss increased the heat of his lips. But he made no gesture to raise her dress or to undress her.

They lay there for a long time. The candle was finished. It sputtered and went out. In the darkness she felt his burning dryness, like desert sand, enveloping her.

Then in this darkness, the Hilda who had made this gesture so many times before was impelled to make it once more, out of her dream and drunkenness of kisses. Her hand fumbled for his belt with the cold silver buckle, felt below the belt at the buttons of his pants, felt his desire.

Suddenly he pushed her away as if she had wounded him. He stood up, reeling a little, and lit another candle. She could not understand what had happened. She saw that he was angry. His eyes had grown fierce. His high cheeks, which seemed always to be smiling, no longer smiled. His mouth was compressed.

"What have I done?" she asked.

He looked like some wild, timid animal that one had done violence to. He looked humiliated, offended, proud, untouchable. She repeated, "What have I done?" She knew that she had done something she ought not to have done. She wanted him to understand that she was innocent.

He smiled now, ironically, at her blindness. He said, "You made the gesture of a whore." A deep shame, a sense of great injury overwhelmed her. The woman in her that had suffered from being forced to act as she did with her other lover, the woman who had been made to betray her real nature so often that it had become a habit, this woman wept now, uncontrollably. The tears did not touch him. She got up, saying, "Even if it is the last time I come here, there is something I want you to know. A woman does not always do what she wants. I was taught by someone . . . someone I have lived with for a number of years and who forced me . . . forced me to act . . ."

Rango listened. She continued. "I suffered at first, I changed my whole nature . . . I . . ." Then she stopped.

Rango sat down next to her. "I understand." He took up his guitar. He played for her. They drank. But he did not touch her. They walked slowly back to where she lived. She dropped exhausted on her bed and fell asleep weeping, not only for the loss of Rango but for the loss of that part of herself she had deformed, changed for love of a man.

The next day Rango was waiting for her at the door of her little hotel. He stood there reading and smoking. When she came out he said simply, "Come and have coffee with me." They sat at the Martinique Café, a café frequented by mulattos, prize fighters, drug addicts. He had chosen a dark corner of the café, and now he bent over her and began to kiss her. He did not pause. He kept her mouth on his and did not move. She dissolved in this kiss.

They walked the streets like Parisian apaches, kissing continuously, making their way to his gypsy cart, half unconscious. Now in full daylight, the place was alive with gypsy women preparing to sell lace in the market. Their men slept. Others were preparing to travel south. Rango said he had always wanted to go with them. But he had a job playing guitar at a night club where they paid him well.

"And now," he said, "I have you."

In the cart he offered her wine and they smoked. And he kissed her again. He raised himself to close the little curtain. And then he undressed her, slowly, taking off the stockings delicately, his big brown hands handling them as if they were gauze, invisible. He stopped to look at her garters. He kissed her feet. He smiled at her. His face was strangely pure, illumined with a youthful joy, and he undressed her as if she were his first woman. He was awkward with her skirt but finally unhooked it, with a curiosity about the way it fastened. More adeptly he raised her sweater above her head, and she was left with only her panties on. He fell on her, kissing her mouth over and over again. Then he took off his own clothes, and fell on her again. As they kissed, his hand gripped her panties and pulled them, and he whispered, "You are so delicate, so small, I cannot believe that you have a sex." He parted her legs only to kiss her. She felt his penis hard against her belly, but he took it and pushed it downwards.

Hilda was amazed to see him do this, push his penis down between his legs, cruelly, thrusting away his desire. It was as if he enjoyed denying himself, while at the same time arousing them both to a breaking point with kissing.

Hilda moaned with the pleasure and the pain of expectancy. He moved over her body, now kissing her mouth, now her sex, so that the shell-like flavor of the sex was brought to her mouth and they mingled together, in his mouth and breath.

But he continued to push away his penis, and when they had worn themselves out with unfulfilled excitement he lay over her and fell asleep like a child, his fists closed, his head on her breast. Now and then he caressed her, mumbling, "It is not possible that you have a sex. You are too delicate and small . . . You are unreal . . ." He kept his hand between her legs. She rested against his body, which was twice the size of hers. She was vibrating so much that she could not sleep.

His body smelled like a precious-wood forest; his hair, like sandalwood, his skin, like cedar. It was as if he had always lived among trees and plants. Lying at his side, deprived of her fulfillment, Hilda felt that the female in her was being taught to submit to the male, to obey his wishes. She felt that he was still punishing her for the gesture she had made, for her impatience, for her first act of leadership. He would rouse and deprive her until he had broken this willfulness in her.

Had he understood that it was involuntary, not truly in her? Whether he had or not, he was blindly determined to break her. Over and over again they met, undressed, lay side by side, kissed and caressed themselves to a frenzy, and each time he pushed his penis downwards and hid it away.

Over and over again she lay passive, showing no desire, no impatience. She was in a state of excitement, which exacerbated all her sensibilities. It was as if she had taken new drugs that made the entire body more alive to caresses, to a touch, to the very air. She felt her dress on her skin like a hand. It seemed to her that everything was touching her like a hand, teasing her breasts, her thighs continuously. She had discovered a new realm, a realm of suspense and watchfulness, of erotic wakefulness such as she had never known.

One day when she was walking with him, she lost the heel of one shoe. He had to carry her. That night he took her, in the candlelight. He was like a demon crouching over her, his hair wild, his charcoal-black eyes burning into hers, his strong penis pounding into her, into the woman whose submission he first demanded, submission to his desire, his hour.

The Chanchiquito

When Laura was about sixteen, she remembered, she was told endless stories of life in Brazil by an uncle who had lived there many years before. He laughed at the inhibitions of Europeans. He said that in Brazil people made love like monkeys, frequently and easily; women were accessible and willing; everybody acknowledged his sensual appetite. He told laughingly of the advice he had given to a friend who was going to Brazil. He had said, "You must take two hats."

"Why?" asked the friend. "I do not want to be loaded with baggage."

"Nevertheless," said Laura's uncle, "you must take two hats with you. The wind may carry one of them off."

"But I can pick it up, can't I?" asked the friend.

"In Brazil," said Laura's uncle, "you cannot lean over or . . ."

He also claimed that in Brazil there existed an animal called the chanchiquito. It looked like a very small pig with an overdeveloped snout. The chanchiquito had a passion for running up the skirts of women and inserting his snout between their legs.

One day, according to her uncle, a very pompous and aristocratic lady arranged a meeting with her lawyer about a will. He was a white-haired, distinguished old man she had known for many years. She was a widow, a very reserved, imposing woman, sumptuously dressed in full satin skirts, with lace collar and cuffs neatly starched and a veil over her face. She sat stiffly like some personage out of an old painting, resting one hand on her parasol, the other on the arm of a chair. They had a quiet and methodical talk together about details of the will.

The old lawyer had once been in love with the lady, but after ten years of courtship had not been able to win her. Now there was always a certain tone of flirtation in their voices, but an imposing, dignified flirtation, more like ancient gallantry.

The meeting took place in the lady's country house. It was very warm and all the doors were open. One could see the hills. The Indian servants were carrying on some celebration. They had surrounded the house with torches. Perhaps frightened by this and unable to escape the circle of fire, a certain small animal scurried along and into the house. Two

minutes later the grand old lady was screaming and contorting herself in her chair, with an attack of hysterics. The servants were called. The witch doctor was called. The witch
doctor and the lady locked themselves in her room together.
When the witch doctor came out, he was carrying the chanchiquito in his arms, and the chanchiquito looked worn, as
though his expedition had almost cost him his life.

This story had frightened Laura—the idea of an animal
burrowing his head between her legs. She was afraid even to
insert her finger. But at the same time the story revealed to
her that between a woman's legs there was room for an animal's long snout.

Then one day during vacation, when she was playing on
the lawn with other friends, and had thrown herself back to
laugh at some story or other, a big police dog was immediately upon her, sniffing and smelling at her clothes, and he
stuck his nose between her legs. Laura screamed and pushed
him off. The sensation had frightened and excited her at the
same time.

And now Laura was lying on a wide, low bed, with her
skirts wrinkled, her hair loose, and rouge spread unevenly
around her lips. By her side lay a man twice her weight and
size who was dressed like a workman, with corduroy trousers
and a leather jacket, which he had opened, showing his bare
neck, not confined by a shirt collar.

She shifted slightly to study him. She could see the high
cheekbone shaped in such a way that he seemed to be always
laughing, and his eyes turned upwards at the corners with
perpetual humor. His hair looked uncombed, and his gestures
were easy as he smoked.

Jan was an artist who laughed at hunger, at work, at slav-
ery, at everything. He preferred to be a tramp rather than lose
his freedom to sleep as late as he liked, to eat what he could

find at the time he wanted it, to paint only when the passion for work took him.

The room was full of his paintings. His palette was covered with paint that was still wet. He had asked Laura to pose for him, and began the work with great eagerness, not seeing her as a person, but observing the shape of her head, the way it seemed to rest on a neck too small for its weight, which gave her an air of almost frightening fragility. She had thrown herself on the bed. As she posed she looked up at the ceiling.

The house was a very old one, with chipped paint and uneven plastering. As she had looked, the roughness of the plaster and its many cracks began to assume shapes. She smiled. There in the jumbled lines and cracks and churned surface she could see all kinds of forms.

She had said to Jan: "When you are finished with your work, I want you to make a drawing for me on the ceiling, of something that is already there, if you can see what I see . . ."

Jan had become curious, and he did not want to work much longer anyway. He had reached the baffling and difficult stage of feet and hands, which he disliked; they perpetually eluded him, so he often wrapped them up in a cloud of formless swathing, like the feet and hands of a cripple, and left the drawing as it was, all body, a body without feet to run away on or hands to caress anyone with.

He turned to the study of the ceiling. To do this he lay back on the bed next to Laura and looked up with keen interest, seeking the forms she had distinguished and following the outlines she indicated with her forefinger.

"See, see, there . . . do you see the woman lying back. . . ?"

Jan rose halfway in the bed—the ceiling was very low in that corner, being an attic room—and with his charcoal began to draw on the plaster. First he sketched the woman's head and her shoulders, but then he found the outline of the legs, which he completed, pointing the toes.

"The skirt, the skirt, I see the skirt," said Laura.

"I see it here," said Jan, drawing a skirt that was quite evidently thrown upwards, leaving her legs and thighs bare. Then Jan darkened the hair around the sex, carefully, as if he were painting grass blade by blade, and added detail to the converging lines of the legs. And there was the woman, reclining on the ceiling without shame, where Jan could look at her with a tiny flame of erotic response, which Laura caught in his intensely blue eyes, and which made her jealous.

To irritate him as he looked at the woman she said, "I see a little piglike animal very near her."

Wrinkling his brow, Jan looked intently to find the outline, but he did not see it. He began to draw at random, following rough ragged edges and confused lines, and what began to take form was a dog who was climbing over the woman, and, with one last ironic stroke of charcoal, he drew in the dog's knifelike sex almost touching the woman's pubic hair.

Laura said, "I see another dog."

"I don't see it," said Jan, and he lay back fully on the bed to admire his drawing, while Laura stood up and began to draw a dog that was climbing over Jan's dog from behind, in the most classical of poses, his shaggy head of hair buried in the other's back as if he were devouring it.

Then with the charcoal Laura began to search for a man. At all cost she wanted a man in this picture. She wanted a man to look at while Jan was looking at the woman with her skirt raised. She began to draw, cautiously, for the lines could not be invented, and if they wavered too much and too faithfully and according to the contours of the plaster, she would have a tree, or a bush, or a monkey. But slowly the man's torso emerged. True, he was legless, and his head was small, but all this was amply compensated for by the largeness of his sex, which was quite obviously in an aggressive mood as he watched the dogs coupling almost on top of the reclining woman.

And then Laura was satisfied and lay back. They both looked at the drawing, laughing, and as they did so, Jan with his big hands still full of drying paint, began to explore under her skirt as if he were drawing, molding the contours with a pencil, touching each line amorously, very gradually traveling up the legs, making sure of having caressed every region and of having gone around every curve.

Laura's legs were half pressed together like the legs of the woman on the ceiling, toes pointed like a ballet dancer's, so when Jan's hand reached her thighs and wanted to be allowed between them, he had to part them with a little force. Laura was nervously resisting, as if she did not want to be anything but the woman on the ceiling, merely exposed, the sex closed, the legs rigid. Jan labored to melt this rigidity, this firmness, and he set about doing it with utmost gentleness and persistence, making magic circles with his fingers on the flesh, as if he could make the blood turn in eddies a little faster, and then yet a little faster.

As Laura continued to look at the woman, she opened her legs. Something touched her hips just as the woman's hips were touched by the stiffened sex of the dog, and she felt as if the dogs were coupling right over her. Jan saw that she was not feeling him but the picture. He shook her with anger, and, as if to punish her he took her with such long, lasting, stubborn emphasis that until she cried to be delivered he did not stop ploughing her. By that time neither one was looking at the ceiling. They were tangled in the bedclothes, half-covered, legs and heads entwined. Thus they fell asleep, and the paints dried on the palette.

Saffron

Fay had been born in New Orleans. When she was sixteen she was courted by a man of forty whom she had always liked for his aristocracy and distinction. Fay was poor. Albert's visits were events to her family. For him their poverty was hastily disguised. He came very much like the liberator, talking about a life Fay had never known, at the other end of the city.

When they were married, Fay was installed like a princess in his house, which was hidden in an immense park. Handsome colored women waited on her. Albert treated her with extreme delicacy.

The first night he did not take her. He maintained that this was proof of love, not to force oneself upon one's wife, but to woo her slowly and lingeringly, until she was prepared and in the mood to be possessed.

He came to her room and merely caressed her. They lay enveloped in the white mosquito netting as within a bridal veil, lay back in the hot night fondling and kissing. Fay felt languid and drugged. He was giving birth to a new woman with every kiss, exposing a new sensibility. Afterwards, when he left her, she lay tossing and unable to sleep. It was as if he had started tiny fires under her skin, tiny currents which kept her awake.

She was exquisitely tormented in this manner for several nights. Being inexperienced, she did not try to bring about a complete embrace. She yielded to this profusion of kisses in her hair, on her neck, shoulders, arms, back, legs . . . Albert took delight in kissing her until she moaned, as if he were now sure of having awakened a particular part of her flesh, and then his mouth moved on.

He discovered the trembling sensibility under the arm, at the nascence of the breasts, the vibrations that ran between the nipples and the sex, and between the sex mouth and the lips, all the mysterious links that roused and stirred places other than the one being kissed, currents running from the roots of the hair to the roots of the spine. Each place he kissed he worshiped with adoring words, observing the dimples at the end of her back, the firmness of her buttocks, the extreme arch of her back, which threw her buttocks outwards—"like a colored woman's," he said.

He encircled her ankles with his fingers, lingered over her feet, which were perfect like her hands, stroked over and over again the smooth statuesque lines of her neck, lost himself in her long heavy hair.

Her eyes were long and narrow like those of a Japanese woman, her mouth full, always half-open. Her breasts heaved as he kissed her and marked her shoulder's sloping line with his teeth. And then as she moaned, he left her, closing the white netting around her carefully, encasing her like a treasure, leaving her with the moisture welling up between her legs.

One night, as usual, she could not sleep. She sat up in her clouded bed, naked. As she rose to look for her kimono and slippers a tiny drop of honey fell from her sex, rolled down her leg, stained the white rug. Fay was baffled at Albert's control, his reserve. How could he subdue his desire and sleep after these kisses and caresses? He had not even completely undressed. She had not seen his body.

She decided to leave her room and walk until she could become calm again. Her entire body was throbbing. She walked slowly down the wide staircase and out into the garden. The perfume of the flowers almost stunned her. The branches fell languidly over her and the mossy paths made her footsteps absolutely silent. She had the feeling that she was dreaming. She walked aimlessly for a long while. And then a sound startled her. It was a moan, a rhythmic moan like a woman's complaining. The light from the moon fell there between the branches and exposed a colored woman lying naked on the moss and Albert over her. Her moans were moans of pleasure. Albert was crouching like a wild animal and pounding against her. He, too, was uttering confused cries; and Fay saw them convulsed under her very eyes by the violent joys.

Neither one saw Fay. She did not cry out. The pain at first paralyzed her. Then she ran back to the house, filled with all the humility of her youth, of her inexperience; she was tortured with doubts of herself. Was it her fault? What had she lacked, what had she failed to do to please Albert? Why had he had to leave her and go to the colored woman? The savage scene haunted her. She blamed herself for falling under the enchantment of his caresses and perhaps not acting as he wanted her to. She felt condemned by her own femininity.

Albert could have taught her. He had said he was wooing her . . . waiting. He had only to whisper a few words. She was ready to obey. She knew he was older and she innocent. She had expected to be taught.

That night Fay became a woman, making a secret of her pain, intent on saving her happiness with Albert, on showing wisdom and subtlety. When he lay at her side she whispered to him, "I wish you would take your clothes off."

He seemed startled, but he consented. Then she saw his youthful, slim body at her side, with his very white hair gleaming, a curious mingling of youth and age. He began to kiss her. As he did so her hand timidly moved towards his body. At first she was frightened. She touched his chest. Then his hips. He continued to kiss her. Her hand reached for his penis, slowly. He made a movement away from it. It was soft. He moved away and began to kiss her between the legs. He was whispering over and over again the same phrase, "You have the body of an angel. It is impossible that such a body should have a sex. You have the body of an angel."

Then anger swept over Fay like a fever, an anger at his moving his penis away from her hand. She sat up, her hair wild about her shoulders, and said, "I am not an angel, Albert. I am a woman. I want you to love me as a woman."

Then came the saddest night Fay had ever known, because Albert tried to possess her and he couldn't. He led her hands to caress him. His penis would harden, he would begin to place it between her legs, and then it would wilt in her hands.

He was tense, silent. She could see the torment on his face. He tried many times. He would say, "Just wait a little while, just wait." He said this so humbly, so gently. Fay lay there, it seemed to her, for the whole of the night, wet, desirous, expectant, and all night he made half finished assaults on her, failing, retreating, kissing her as if in atonement. Then Fay sobbed.

This scene was repeated for two or three nights, and then Albert no longer came to her room.

And almost every day Fay saw shadows in the garden, shadows embracing. She was afraid to move from her room. The house was completely carpeted and noiseless, and as she walked up the stairs once she caught sight of Albert climbing behind one of the colored girls and running his hand under her voluminous skirt.

Fay became obsessed with the sounds of the moaning. It seemed to her that she heard it continuously. Once she went to the colored girls' rooms, which were in a separate little house, and listened. She could hear the moans she had heard in the park. She broke into tears. A door opened. It was not Albert who came out but one of the colored gardeners. He found Fay sobbing there.

Eventually Albert took her, under the most unusual circumstances. They were going to give a party for Spanish friends. Although she seldom shopped, Fay went to the city to get a particular saffron for the rice, a very extraordinary brand that had just arrived on a ship from Spain. She enjoyed buying the saffron, freshly unloaded. She had always liked smells, the smells of the wharves, and warehouses. When the little packages of saffron were handed to her, she tucked them in her bag, which she carried against her breast, under her arm. The smell was powerful, it seeped into her clothes, her hands, her very body.

When she arrived home Albert was waiting for her. He came towards the car and lifted her out of it, playfully, laughing. As he did so, she brushed with her full weight against him and he exclaimed, "You smell of saffron!"

She saw a curious brilliance in his eyes, as he pressed his face against her breasts smelling her. Then he kissed her. He followed her into her bedroom, where she threw her bag on the bed. The bag opened. The smell of saffron filled the room. Albert made her lie on the bed, fully dressed, and without kisses or caresses, took her.

Afterwards he said happily, "You smell like a colored woman." And the spell was broken.

Mandra

The illumined skyscrapers shine like Christmas trees. I have been invited to stay with rich friends at the Plaza. The luxury lulls me, but I lie in a soft bed sick with ennui, like a flower in a hothouse. My feet rest on soft carpets. New York gives me a fever—the great Babylonian city.

I see Lillian. I no longer love her. There are those who

dance and those who twist themselves into knots. I like those who flow and dance. I will see Mary again. Perhaps this time I will not be timid. I remember when she came to Saint-Tropez one day and we met casually at a café. She invited me to come to her room in the evening.

My lover, Marcel, had to go home that night; he lived quite far away. I was free. I left him at eleven o'clock and went to see Mary. I was wearing my flounced Spanish cretonne dress and a flower in my hair, and I was all bronzed by the sun and feeling beautiful.

When I arrived, Mary was lying on her bed cold-creaming her face, her legs and her shoulders because she had been lying on the beach. She was rubbing cream into her neck, her throat—she was covered with cream.

This disappointed me. I sat at the foot of her bed and we talked. I lost my desire to kiss her. She was running away from her husband. She had married him only to be protected. She had never really loved men but women. At the beginning of her marriage, she had told him all sorts of stories about herself that she should not have told him—how she had been a dancer on Broadway and slept with men when she was short of money; how she even went to a whorehouse and earned money there; how she met a man who fell in love with her and kept her for a few years. Her husband never recovered from these stories. They awakened his jealousy and doubts, and their life together had become intolerable.

The day after we met, she left Saint-Tropez, and I was filled with regrets for not having kissed her. Now I was about to see her again.

In New York I unfold my wings of vanity and coquetry. Mary is as lovely as ever and seems much moved by me. She is all curves, softness. Her eyes are wide and liquid; her cheeks, luminous. Her mouth is full; her hair blond, and luxu-

riant. She is slow, passive, lethargic. We go to the movies together. In the dark she takes my hand.

She is being analyzed and has discovered what I sensed
long ago: that she has never known a real orgasm, at thirty-
four, after a sexual life that only an expert accountant could
keep track of. I am discovering her pretenses. She is always
smiling, gay, but underneath she feels unreal, remote, de-
tached from experience. She acts as if she were asleep. She is
trying to awaken by falling into bed with anyone who invites
her.

Mary says, "It is very hard to talk about sex, I am so
ashamed." She is not ashamed of doing anything at all, but
she cannot talk about it. She can talk to me. We sit for hours
in perfumed places where there is music. She likes places
where actors go.

There is a current of attraction between us, purely physical. We are always on the verge of getting into bed together.
But she is never free in the evenings. She will not let me meet
her husband. She is afraid I will seduce him.

She fascinates me because sensuality pours from her. At
eight years old she was already having a Lesbian affair with
an older cousin.

We both share the love of finery, perfume and luxury.
She is so lazy, languid—purely a plant, really. I have never
seen a woman more yielding. She says that she always expects
to find the man who will arouse her. She has to live in a sexual
atmosphere even when she feels nothing. It is her climate.
Her favorite statement is, "At that time, I was sleeping
around with everybody."

If we speak of Paris and of people we knew there, she always says, "I don't know him. I didn't sleep with him." Or,
"Oh, yes, he was wonderful in bed."

I have never once heard of her resisting—this, coupled
with frigidity! She deceives everybody, including herself. She

looks so wet and open that men think she is continuously in a
state of near orgasm. But it is not true. The actress in her appears cheerful and calm, and inside she is going to pieces. She
drinks and can sleep only by taking drugs. She always comes
to me eating candy, like a schoolgirl. She looks about twenty.
Her coat is open, her hat is in her hand. Her hair is loose.

One day she falls on my bed and knocks off her shoes.
She looks at her legs and says, "They are too thick. They are
like Renoir legs, I was told once in Paris."

"But I love them," I say, "I love them."

"Do you like my new stockings?" She raises her skirt to
show me.

She asks for a whiskey. Then she decides that she will
take a bath. She borrows my kimono. I know that she is trying
to tempt me. She comes out of the bathroom still humid, leaving the kimono open. Her legs are always held a little apart.
She looks so much as if she were about to have an orgasm that
one cannot help feeling: only one little caress will drive her
wild. As she sits on the edge of my bed to put on her stockings, I cannot withhold any longer. I kneel in front of her and
put my hand on the hair between her legs. I stroke it gently,
gently, and I say, "The little silver fox, the little silver fox. So
soft and beautiful. Oh, Mary, I can't believe that you do not
feel anything there, inside."

She seems on the verge of feeling, the way her flesh looks,
open like a flower, the way her legs are spread. Her mouth is
so wet, so inviting, the lips of her sex must be the same. She
parts her legs and lets me look at it. I touch it gently and
spread the lips to see if they are moist. She feels it when I
touch her clitoris, but I want her to feel the bigger orgasm.

I kiss her clitoris, still wet from the bath; her pubic hair,
still damp as seaweed. Her sex tastes like a seashell, a wonderful, fresh, salty seashell. Oh, Mary! My fingers work more
quickly, she falls back on the bed, offering her whole sex to

me, open and moist, like a camellia, like rose petals, like vel-
vet, satin. It is rosy and new, as if no one had ever touched it.
It is like the sex of a young girl.

Her legs hang over the side of the bed. Her sex is open; I
can bite into it, kiss it, insert my tongue. She does not move.
The little clitoris stiffens like a nipple. My head between her
two legs is caught in the most delicious vise of silky, salty
flesh.

My hands travel upwards to her heavy breasts, caress
them. She begins to moan a little. Now her hands travel
downwards and join mine in caressing her own sex. She likes
to be touched at the mouth of her sex, below the clitoris. She
touches the place with me. It is there I would like to push in a
penis and move until I make her scream with pleasure. I put
my tongue at the opening and push it in as far as it will go. I
take her ass in my two hands, like a big fruit, and push it upwards, and while my tongue is playing there in the mouth of
her sex, my fingers press into the flesh of her ass, travel
around its firmness, into its curve, and my forefinger feels the
little mouth of her anus and pushes in gently.

Suddenly Mary gives a start—as if I have touched off an
electric spark. She moves to enclose my finger. I press it farther, all the while moving my tongue inside of her sex. She
begins to moan, to undulate.

When she sinks downwards she feels my flicking finger,
when she rises upwards she meets my flicking tongue. With
every move, she feels my quickening rhythm, until she has a
long spasm and begins to moan like a pigeon. With my finger
I feel the palpitation of pleasure, going once, twice, thrice,
beating ecstatically.

She falls over, panting. "Oh, Mandra, what have you
done to me, what have you done to me!" She kisses me, drink-
ing the salty moisture from my mouth. Her breasts fall against

me as she holds me, saying again, "Oh, Mandra, what have you done . . ."

I am invited one night to the apartment of a young society couple, the H's. It is like being on a boat because it is near the East River and the barges pass while we talk, the river is alive. Miriam is a delight to look at, a Brunhilde, full-breasted, with sparkling hair, a voice that lures you to her. Her husband, Paul, is small and of the race of the imps, not a man but a faun—a lyrical animal, quick and humorous. He thinks I am beautiful. He treats me like an objet d'art. The black butler opens the door. Paul exclaims over me, my Goyaesque hood, the red flower in my hair, and hurries me into the salon to display me. Miriam is sitting cross-legged on a purple satin divan. She is a natural beauty, whereas I, an artificial one, need a setting and warmth to bloom success-fully.

Their apartment is full of furnishings I find individually ugly—silver candelabra, tables with nooks for trailing flowers, enormous mulberry satin poufs, rococo objects, things full of chic, collected with snobbish playfulness, as if to say "We can make fun of everything created by fashion, we are above it all."

Everything is touched with aristocratic impudence, through which I can sense the H's fabulous life in Rome, Florence; Miriam's frequent appearances in *Vogue* wearing Chanel dresses; the pompousness of their families; their efforts to be elegantly bohemian; and their obsession with the word that is the key to society—everything must be "amusing."

Miriam calls me into her bedroom to show me a new bathing suit she has bought in Paris. For this, she undresses herself completely, and then takes the long piece of material and begins rolling it around herself like the primitive draping of the Balinese.

Her beauty goes to my head. She undrapes herself, walks naked around the room, and then says, "I wish I looked like you. You are so exquisite and dainty. I am so big."

"But that's just why I like you, Miriam."

"Oh, your perfume, Mandra."

She pushes her face into my shoulder under my hair and smells my skin.

I place my hand on her shoulder.

"You're the most beautiful woman I've ever seen, Miriam."

Paul is calling out to us, "When are you going to finish talking about clothes in there? I'm bored!"

Miriam replies, "We're coming." And she dresses quickly in slacks. When she comes out Paul says, "And now you're dressed to stay at home, and I want to take you to hear the String Man. He sings the most marvelous songs about a string and finally hangs himself on it."

Miriam says, "Oh, all right. I'll get dressed." And she goes into the bathroom.

I stay behind with Paul, but soon Miriam calls me. "Mandra, come in here and talk to me."

I think, by this time she will be half-dressed, but no, she is standing naked in the bathroom, powdering and fixing her face.

She is as opulent as a burlesque queen. As she stands on her toes to lean towards the mirror and paint her eyelashes more carefully, I am again affected by her body. I come up behind her and watch her.

I feel a little timid. She isn't as inviting as Mary. She is, in fact, sexless, like the women at the beach or at the Turkish bath, who think nothing of their nakedness. I try a light kiss on her shoulder. She smiles at me and says, "I wish Paul were not so irritable. I would have liked to try the bathing suit on you. I would love to see you wearing it." She returns my kiss, on the mouth, taking care not to disturb her lipstick outline. I do not know what to do next. I want to take hold of her. I stay near her.

Then Paul comes into the bathroom without knocking and says, "Miriam, how can you walk around like this? You mustn't mind, Mandra. It is a habit with her. She is possessed with the need to go around without clothes. Get dressed, Miriam."

Miriam goes into her room and slips on a dress, with nothing underneath, then a fox cape, and says, "I'm ready."

In the car she places her hand over mine. Then she draws my hand under the fur, into a pocket of the dress, and I find myself touching her sex. We drive on in the dark.

Miriam says she wants to drive through the park first. She wants air. Paul wants to go directly to the nightclub, but he gives in and we drive through the park, I with my hand on Miriam's sex, fondling it and feeling my own excitement gaining so that I can hardly talk.

Miriam talks, wittily, continuously. I think to myself, "You won't be able to go on talking in a little while." But she does, all the time that I am caressing her in the dark, beneath the satin and the fur. I can feel her moving upwards to my touch, opening her legs a little so I can fit my entire hand between her legs. Then she grows tense under my fingers, stretching herself, and I know she is taking her pleasure. It is contagious. I feel my own orgasm without even being touched.

I am so wet that I am afraid it will show through my dress. And it must show through Miriam's dress, too. We both keep our coats on as we go into the nightclub.

Miriam's eyes are brilliant, deep. Paul leaves us for a while and we go into the ladies' room. This time Miriam kisses my mouth fully, boldly. We arrange ourselves and return to the table.

Runaway

Pierre was sharing an apartment with a much younger man, Jean. One day Jean brought home a young girl he had found wandering in the streets. He had seen that she was not a prostitute.

She was barely sixteen, with close-cropped hair worn like a boy's, a youthfully formed figure, two little sharply pointed breasts. She had responded to Jean's words immediately but in a dazed fashion. She said, "I have run away from home."

"And where are you going now? Have you got money?"

"No, I have no money, and no place to sleep."

"Then come with me," said Jean. "I shall make you dinner and give you a room." She followed him with incredible docility.

"What is your name?"

"Jeanette."

"Oh, we fit well together. I am Jean."

There were two bedrooms in the apartment, with a double bed in each. At first Jean had really intended to rescue the girl, and to go to sleep in Pierre's bed. Pierre had not come home. He felt no desire, but a kind of pity for her forlorn, lost air. He made dinner for her. Then she said she was sleepy. Jean gave her a pair of his pajamas, showed her into his room and left.

Soon after he had gone into Pierre's room, he heard her calling to him. She sat up in bed like a weary child and made him sit beside her. She asked him to kiss her goodnight. Her lips were inexperienced. She gave him a gentle, innocent kiss, but this aroused Jean. He made the kiss last and pushed his tongue into her soft little mouth. She permitted this with the same docility she had shown in coming home with him.

Then Jean became more aroused. He stretched himself beside her. She seemed to like it. He was a little frightened by her youthfulness, but he could not believe that she was yet a virgin. The way she kissed was no proof for him. He had known many women who did not know how to kiss but who had known how to clutch at a man in other ways and receive him with great hospitality.

He began to teach her how to kiss. He said to her, "Give me your tongue as I gave you mine." She obeyed.

"Do you like it?" he asked. She nodded her head.

Then, as he lay back watching her, she raised herself on her elbow and very seriously stretched out her tongue and placed it between Jean's lips.

This enchanted him. She was a good pupil. He made her move it and flick it. They remained glued together for a long time before he attempted any other caress. Then he explored her little breasts. She responded to his little pinchings and kissing.

"You never kissed a man before?" he asked her incredulously.

"No," said the young girl, very seriously. "But I always wanted to. That is why I ran away. I knew my mother would continue to hide me. Meanwhile she was receiving men all the time. I heard them. My mother is quite beautiful, and men often came and locked themselves in with her. But she would never let me see them, or even let me go out alone. And I wanted to have a few men to myself."

"A few men," said Jean laughing. "One is not enough?"

"I don't know yet," she said with the same seriousness. "I will have to see."

Then Jean turned his whole attention to Jeanette's firm and pointed little breasts. He kissed them and fondled them. Jeanette was watching him with great interest. Then when he stopped to rest himself, she suddenly unbuttoned his shirt, and laid her fresh breasts against his chest and rubbed herself against it exactly like a languorous, voluptuous cat. Jean was amazed at her talent for lovemaking. She was progressing fast. Her nipples had known just how to touch his own, just how to rub against his chest and excite him.

So now he uncovered her and began to unfasten the cord of her pajamas. But at this point she asked him to turn out the light.

Pierre came home about midnight, and as he walked past the room he heard the moaning sounds of a woman, which he recognized as sounds of pleasure. He stopped. He could imagine the scene behind the door. The moans were rhythmic, then at times like the cooing of doves. Pierre could not help listening.

Then the next day Jean told him about Jeanette. He said, "You know, I thought she was just a young girl, and she was . . . she was a virgin, but you have never seen such an aptitude for love. She is insatiable. She has already worn me out."

Then he went out to work, and was gone the whole day. Pierre remained in the apartment. At noon Jeanette appeared quite timidly and asked if she was going to have lunch. So they had lunch together. Then after lunch she disappeared until Jean came home. The same thing happened the next day. And the next. She was as quiet as a mouse. But every night Pierre heard the moaning and crooning, the dove-cooing behind the door. After eight days, he noticed that Jean was growing tired. Jean was twice Jeanette's age to begin with, and then Jeanette, keeping her mother in mind, must have been seeking to outdo her.

On the ninth day Jean stayed out all night. Jeanette came to wake Pierre. She was alarmed. She thought Jean had met with an accident. But Pierre had guessed the truth. Indeed, Jean was already tired of her and wanted to inform her mother of her whereabouts. But he had not been able to extract the address from Jeanette. So he merely stayed away.

Pierre tried to console Jeanette as best he could, then went back to sleep. She wandered aimlessly about the apartment, picking up books and dropping them, trying to eat, telephoning the police. At all hours of the night she entered Pierre's room to talk about her anxieties, and she remained gazing at him wistfully, helplessly.

Finally she dared to ask him, "Do you think Jean does not want me about anymore? Do you think I should go away?"

"I think you should return home," said Pierre, weary and sleepy and indifferent to the young girl.

But the next day she was still there, and something happened to disturb his indifference.

Jeanette sat at the end of his bed to talk to him. She was wearing a very thin dress that seemed like a light sachet around her, merely a cover to hold the perfume of her body. A composite perfume, so strong and penetrating, Pierre could catch all its nuances—the bitter, strong odor of the hair; the few drops of perspiration on her neck, under her breasts, under her arms; her breath, both acid and sweet, like some mixture of lemon and honey; and beneath all this the odor of her femininity, which the summer heat wakened as it awakened the smell of flowers.

He became fully aware of his own body, feeling the caress of his pajamas on his skin, aware that they were open at the chest and that she could perhaps smell his odor as he was smelling hers.

His desire suddenly asserted itself, violently. He pulled Jeanette towards him. He made her slide beside him, and he felt her body through the thin dress. But at the same moment he remembered how Jean had made her moan and croon by the hour, and he wondered if he could do it as well. Never before had he been so near to another man making love or overheard the sounds of a woman being exhausted by pleasure. He had no reason to doubt his own power. He had ample proofs of his success as a good and satisfying lover. But this time, as he began to caress Jeanette, a doubt took hold of him —such a fear that his desire died.

Jeanette was amazed to see Pierre grown suddenly limp in the very middle of his fervent caresses. She felt contempt. She was too inexperienced to think that this might happen to any man in certain circumstances, so she did nothing to revive their lovemaking. She lay back, sighed and looked at the ceiling. Then Pierre kissed her mouth, and this she enjoyed. He lifted the light dress, looked at her young legs, pulled down the round garters. The sight of the stocking beginning to roll down and the tiny white panties she wore, the smallness of the sex he felt under his fingers, aroused him again, giving him such a desire to take her and do violence to her, so yielding and moist. He pushed his powerful sex into her and felt the tightness. This enchanted him. Like a sheath, her sex closed around his penis, softly and caressingly.

He felt his power coming back to him, his usual power and deftness. He knew by each move she made where she wanted to be touched. When she pressed against him, he covered her little round buttocks with his warm hands, and his finger touched the orifice. She leaped under his touch but made no sound.

And Pierre was waiting for this sound, a sound of approval, encouragement. No sound came from Jeanette. Pierre listened for it while he continued to pound into her.

Then he stopped, half withdrew his penis, and with the tip of it alone, he circled the opening of her little rosy sex.

She smiled at him and abandoned herself, but she still did not utter a sound. Wasn't she enjoying herself? What was it that Jean did to her that wrung such shrieks of pleasure from her? He tried all his positions. He raised her towards him by the middle of her body, brought her sex up to him, and he kneeled to better push into her, but she made no sound. He turned her over, and took her from behind. His hands were everywhere. She was panting and moist, but silent. Pierre touched her little ass, caressed her small breasts, bit into her lips, kissed her sex, thrust his sex into her violently and then softly turned and churned in her, but still she remained silent.

In desperation he said, "Say when you want it, say when you want it."

"Come now," she said immediately, as if she had been waiting for him to do it.

"Do you want it," he asked again, filled with doubts.

"Yes," she said, but her passivity made him uncertain. He lost all his desire to come, to enjoy her. His desire died inside of her. He saw an expression of disappointment in her face.

It was she who said, "I suppose I'm not as attractive to you as other women."

Pierre was surprised. "Of course you are attractive to me, but you did not seem to be enjoying yourself and that stopped me."

"I was enjoying myself," said Jeanette, startled. "Of course I was. I was only afraid of Jean's coming and of his hearing me. I thought, if he comes and finds me here, at least if he does not hear me he may think you took me against my will. But if he hears me, he will know I enjoy it and be hurt, for he is the one who keeps saying to me, 'So you like it, so you like it, say so then, go on, speak, cry out, you like it, eh? It gets you, you enjoy it, enjoy it then, *say* so, *speak,* how does it feel?' I can't tell him *how* it feels, but it makes me cry out and then he is happy and that excites him."

Jean should have known what would happen between Jeanette and Pierre while he was out, but he did not believe Pierre could take a real interest in her; she was too much of a child. He was immensely surprised when he returned and found that Jeanette had stayed on and that Pierre was perfectly willing to console her, to take her out.

Pierre took pleasure in buying her clothes. For this purpose he accompanied her to the shops and waited as she tried on clothes inside the little booths provided for this. He delighted in seeing through a slit of the hastily drawn curtains not only Jeanette, her girlish body slipping in and out of dresses, but other women too. He would sit quietly in a chair facing the dressing rooms, smoking. He could see portions of

shoulders, bare backs, legs, flitting behind the curtains. And
Jeanette's gratitude for the clothes he gave her took the form
of a coquetry comparable only to the mannerisms of strip-
teasers. She could hardly wait to be out of the shop to glue
herself to him as they walked, saying, "Look at me. Isn't it
beautiful?" And she would thrust her breasts out provoca-
tively.

As soon as they got into a taxi she wanted him to touch
the material, to approve the buttons, to straighten the neck-
line. She stretched her body voluptuously, to see how closely
the dress fit her; she caressed the material as if it were her
own skin.

As eager as she had been to wear the dress, she now
seemed eager to take it off, to have it handled by Pierre, to
have it wrinkled, to have it baptized by his desire.

She moved against him, inside of the new dress, which
made him keenly aware of her aliveness. And when finally
they got home, she wanted to be locked in his room with him,
to have him appropriate the dress as much as he had her
body, not satisfied until by friction, rubbing, undulations,
Pierre felt the urge to tear the dress off her. When this was
done, she did not remain in his arms, but went all over the
room in her underwear, brushing her hair, powdering her face
and acting as if that was all she intended to remove, and
Pierre would have to be content with her as she was.

She still wore her high-heeled shoes, her stockings, her
garters, and the flesh showed between the garters and the beginning of her panties, and again between her waist and the
little brassiere.

After a moment Pierre tried to hold her. He wanted to
undress her. He managed only to unfasten the brassiere when
she slipped out of his arms again to perform a little dance for
him. All the steps she knew she wanted to do for him. Pierre
admired her lightness.

He caught her as she passed, but she refused to let him touch her panties. She let him take off only her stockings and shoes. But at this moment she heard Jean enter.

As she was, she leaped out of Pierre's room and rushed to meet him. Jean saw her flinging herself into his arms, naked but for the panties. Then he saw Pierre, who had followed her, angry to be deprived of his satisfaction, angry that she should have preferred Jean to him.

Jean understood. But he had no desire for Jeanette. He wanted to be free of her. So he rebuffed her, and left them.

Then Jeanette turned on Pierre. Pierre tried to calm her. She remained angry. She began to pack, to dress, to leave.

Pierre barred her way, carried her to his room and flung her on the bed.

He would have her this time, at all cost. The struggle was pleasant, his rough suit against her skin, his buttons against her tender breasts, his shoes against her naked feet. In all this mixture of hardness and softness, coldness and warmth, rigidity and yielding, Jeanette felt for the first time Pierre as master. He sensed this. He tore off her panties, discovered her moisture.

And then he was taken with a diabolical desire to hurt her. He inserted only his finger. When he had moved this finger until Jeanette pleaded to be satisfied and rolled with excitement, he stopped.

Before her astonished face, he took hold of his erect penis and caressed it, giving himself all the pleasure he could extract, sometimes using only two fingers around the tip of it, sometimes the whole hand, and Jeanette could see every contraction and expansion. It was as if he held a palpitating bird in his hand, a captive bird that tried to leap at her but that Pierre kept for his own pleasure. She gazed at Pierre's penis, fascinated. She drew her face nearer. But his anger at her for darting out of the room to Jean was still fresh in him.

She knelt in front of him. Although she was throbbing between the legs, she felt if she could at least kiss his penis she might satisfy her desire. Pierre let her kneel. He seemed about to offer his penis to her mouth, but he did not. He continued to massage it, angrily enjoying his own motions, as if to say, "I don't need you."

Jeanette threw herself on the bed and became hysterical. Her wild gestures, the way she pressed her head back into the pillow so she could no longer see Pierre caressing himself, the way her body lay arched upwards—all of this stirred Pierre. But still he did not give her his penis. Instead, he buried his face between her legs. Jeanette fell back and grew quieter. She murmured softly.

Pierre's mouth gathered the fresh foam between her legs, but he would not let her reach her pleasure. He teased her. As soon as he felt the rhythm of her pleasure starting he stopped. He held her legs apart. His hair fell on her belly and caressed her. His left hand reached for one of her breasts. Jeanette lay almost swooning. He knew now that Jean could come in and she would not notice him. Jean could even make love to her, and she would not notice him. She was completely under the spell of Pierre's fingers, awaiting pleasure from him. When finally his erect penis touched her soft body, it was as if he had burned her; she trembled. He had never seen her body so abandoned, so unconscious of all but the desire to be taken and satisfied. She bloomed under his caresses, no longer the girl but the woman already being born.